THE *hawk*
THAT DARE NOT
hunt
BY DAY

SCOTT O'DELL

journeyforth®

Greenville, South Carolina

Visit bjupress.com to access a free discussion guide.

The Hawk That Dare Not Hunt by Day
Scott O'Dell

Edited by Carolyn Cooper
Designed by Craig Oesterling
Cover Photo by Unusual Films

© 1975 by Scott O'Dell

ISBN 978-0-89084-368-0
Printed in the United States of America

20   19   18

Publisher's Note

A man must believe or die—that is the law.

To many, such laws could exist only in the dictatorships of the present. Yet the setting for *The Hawk That Dare Not Hunt by Day* is Europe in the early 1500s.

In most countries, a close link bound together the papal clergyman and the politician. Indeed, most people gave the papacy supremacy over human governments. Men such as William Tyndale, who were ready to insist that the individual alone was responsible before God for his beliefs, were in constant danger of losing money, livelihood, personal freedom, and life itself in the war against the bondage imposed on man in the name of the Roman Catholic church of the sixteenth century.

You will notice as you read how their way of life was quite different back then—even the ways in which they thought. To be educated was a luxury, not a way of life as it is today. Common people and royalty alike were subject to fears that we would regard as fantastical. They regarded as true the legends that they heard about the "fey folk," "wee folk" such as naiads, dryads, and mermaids interfering with or blessing mere mortals.

Concerning their ethics, men who smuggled goods under the king's nose were still considered by many as honorable merchants whose word was as good as a signed contract. Law enforcement was often a case of the stronger overcoming the weaker, and if the men of the law should be beaten and turned out, they often would not come back for a second try against men they wanted to throw into prison. Hearings, trials, etc., were things for criminals of state who had attracted public notice, not for the common man.

And you will notice that the people were much earthier. They lived through one plague after another—also through famine, unclean housing, cramped quarters. Baths were infrequent. The same clothes were often worn until they fell apart. In jails people were crowded together and left without food.

Because of the unclean conditions, disease was rife through much of old Europe, and the water was impure. The buying and selling of wine, which purified water, was common and not looked upon with disfavor, although of course drunkenness was frowned upon and could be punished with a jailing or fine. When Tyndale agreed to have his Bibles hidden in wine barrels, it was because he knew that barrels of wine were commonly shipped across the English Channel for necessary use in England. Tyndale did not approve of drunkenness, and if his life had fit him into a different context, we would—no doubt—have found him a leader in condemning the distillation of alcoholic beverages for the purpose of drinking at leisure and dulling the senses.

Death in the sixteenth century was common, and man's view of death has changed quite a bit in the last four hundred years. Pre-Renaissance men made a strong separation in their minds between the body and the soul. The body was a mere shell. Men in those days favored strong punishments, long fasts, and hard living as a means of keeping the body under. On the other hand, the soul was plied with Holy Days, relics, sacraments, prayers, and subservience to the Church. Tyndale's and Luther's preachings brought about moderation on the first and a reformation of the treatment of the second. But in the meantime, the modern reader might feel a little shocked at the seemingly callous way that the people treated the dead—committing them to common graves and dragging them about. It is important to remember that—even more to the man of the sixteenth century than to the Christian of today—the body was just a shell, useless when the soul had abandoned it. Lavish funerals, elaborate coffins, exaggerated care for the dead—this kind of treatment belonged to the kings and dukes, popes and cardinals who sought to be made immortal on earth by monuments and embalming fluids.

The places and conditions described in this book are real, and some of the events really occurred. But of course this book is historical fiction. It does not present itself as a factual statement of all the details of Tyndale's life. Some of the characters are entirely fictional. What is true is that Mr. O'Dell has captured for us the quiet and gentle greatness of William Tyndale—his vision that put a Bible into the hands of the common plowboys of England, his fearlessness that allowed him to play tag with death while he carried on his great work, and most of all, his walk with his great God who gave him a great compassion for the simple people of England.

NORTH SEA

ENGLANDE

LONDON
Greenwich
Gravesend
Mouth of the Thames
Ramsgate

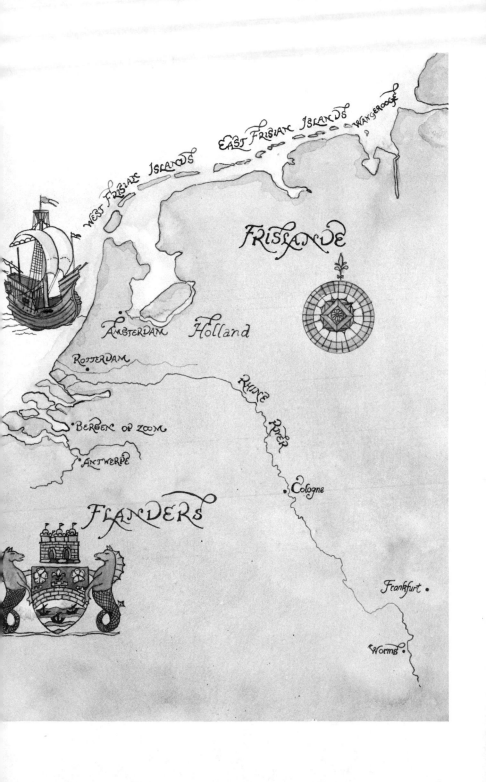

BOOK ONE

Chapter 1

It was the month of April and time for flowers, but around me, wherever my eyes wandered, there was no sign of spring. The far shore of the Thames was only a thin gray line against a lowering sky. Beyond the near shore the red roofs and the gray walls of London had a wintry look. Gusts of wind swept the ship's bare masts and frayed rigging.

We lay anchored in midriver, close upon the bridge, waiting for the tide to turn.

The bridge surged with handcarts and horsecarts and hundreds of people going about their morning chores. Yet there was scarcely a murmur from them. The pilings of the bridge, for some reason called starlings, were so massive and close together that the tide fighting its way to the sea swept against them with an uproar that drowned out all sounds, even the church bells of London.

We stood on deck, I and the captain, my Uncle Jack, patiently waiting for the tide. The bridge looming above us, with its hundreds of shops, back to back and side to side, all helter-skelter, looked like the cells of a giant beehive.

Off to our right was a wherry with two men sculling back and forth against the tide. One of them, a grim-faced fellow with a long, pale nose, we knew by sight. Indeed, every time my Uncle Jack went ashore, he was apt to follow my uncle around, suddenly appearing in odd places, then silently slipping away.

Just above us a mournful-looking little man squeezed through a hole between two shops and shouted down to us, "Fresh eels. Nice fresh eels caught today," and brandished one of his wares at us.

My Uncle Jack said, "Would you like one for supper? An eel might taste good. Good, eh?"

"I'd prefer a large chine of beef."

"What if we partake of both," Uncle Jack said, motioning the monger to toss down one of his small eels. "To celebrate our arrival. To celebrate, eh?"

"To celebrate our being alive," I added. "It was nip and tuck for a while last night."

"Aye, it was. Especially at that moment when the mainmast split and came close to crashing down. The mainmast, mind you. Perhaps we should celebrate with a large eel instead of a small eel. A big time."

Uncle Jack again called to the monger, holding his hands apart to indicate a larger size.

It was a long throw from bridge to ship, a good way out and a good way down, but the monger managed it. The eel was freshly caught, as he had claimed, for despite its being flung down upon the deck from afar, it wiggled mightily and was difficult to subdue.

"Slippery as our friend of the pale nose," the captain said, placing his boot upon the eel's head. "Slippery."

Uncle Jack was a thick-set man with pawlike hands and powerful legs. As he stepped hard upon the eel's head, there was a glint in his eye that said, "One of these days, when we meet again, I'll do the same to our curious friend."

"But what if our friend turns out to be an agent of the Crown?" I humbly asked, reading his thought. "Which, most likely, he is. That or an agent of Thomas More's. Possibly a searcher."

"It makes no difference," Uncle Jack answered. "An agent of one or the other, King or Chancellor. Or searcher in the pay of customs. The customs. A searcher. No matter, eh?"

This was a brave but foolish remark. The mere threat could land him in jail and, if he dared carry it out, surely cost him an ear or an eye.

"King Henry's in a pawky mood," I said. "If the curious gentleman is indeed one of the King's agents, this is not the time to arouse him."

In addition to Henry's past and current troubles with the Emperor, the Pope, and his wife, Catherine, he had just experienced, scarcely a month before, a close brush with death.

In a joust with the Duke of Suffolk, he had entered the list with the visor of his helmet open. Horrified spectators had shouted to Suffolk to hold back his lance, but he could neither see that the King's face was unprotected nor hear the dire warnings. The Duke's lance struck and shattered against the King's helmet, within a bare inch of his exposed face.

Furthermore and more recently, King Henry had fallen from his horse headfirst into a muddy river bank, nearly dying of suffocation ere he was reached.

"This is not the moment for such things," I reminded him again, at the same time pointing over his shoulder.

A short distance beyond where the eelmonger stood, near the entrance to the bridge, was a brace of pike poles and on each of the poles was impaled a severed head. The heads had once belonged to the heretics William Stokes and Reginald Lane. Two months before, when we were last in London, the heads of these two gentlemen were quite lifelike, having been freshly pickled and placed on display.

"They have not weathered well," Uncle Jack said. "A poor job from the pickler, eh?"

In truth, they hadn't weathered well, being badly wrinkled and of a sooty color, their long beards bedraggled.

Uncle Jack himself possessed a beard. It was black, square-cut, and rested upon his chest like a neat block of wood. Gazing at the bedraggled beards, he unconsciously began to finger his own. I presume a cautionary thought ran through his mind at that moment, for he suddenly turned away and ordered me to gather up the eel and take it along to the galley.

On the way back I paused at my locker, stuffed a carefully wrapped package of printed matter into my doublet, and donned a heavy coat. I returned to the deck as the tide turned and, taking the wheel, maneuvered the *Black Pearl* under the bridge.

As I headed toward the Steelyard dock, I noticed that a sparrow was tugging away at what was left of Reginald Lane's beard. In a moment the bird flew low over my head, a long hair trailing from its beak.

The nest-building sparrow was the only sign of spring that I saw that morning.

Chapter 2

The *Black Pearl* carried a mixed cargo.

Officially, in our hold were lead and black copper for the English arsenals at Ainsworth, a small amount of mercury from the Almadén mines, a hundred lengths of blue velvet from Venice and Carcassonne, six hogsheads of Malacca cinnamon, four of Spanish salt, and fifty wheels of cheese from Antwerp.

Unofficially, Uncle Jack was in possession of a hundred lengths of Parisian silks and two fine emeralds from Amsterdam.

In my possession, concealed inside my doublet, were twenty copies of Martin Luther's latest manifesto, fresh from the presses in Wittenberg. In my locker were two hundred more of the same.

When we anchored near the Steelyard dock and the customs men came aboard, I bade them a right good morning and slipped quietly ashore. Uncle Jack, being captain and owner, was forced to remain aboard until the inspection was completed and the manifest signed.

Perhaps I should explain about the Steelyard.

It was, in a manner of speaking, a city within a city. It sat on the banks of the river, at the foot of Cannon Street, a two-storied structure of hewn stone. From the outside it looked much like a fortress, with a squat tower, part of a battlement, and an enormous iron-banded gate that was closed and guarded at night.

The yard belonged to a group of prosperous Hansa merchants. Here these foreigners shipped and sold goods. Most of them resided within its walls, having many facilities for comfortable, even luxurious living. Furthermore, they were protected by the King and enjoyed privileges that even the citizens of London did not possess. In return, English merchants across the channel in Antwerp and Amsterdam owned similar establishments, which were also protected, and held special privileges.

4

The Steelyard's ground floor was arranged for the display of goods. Toward this part of the yard, and to the establishment of Hans Schwertzfeger, I now made my way.

Herr Schwertzfeger was one of the least prosperous of the German merchants, yet he turned a tidy profit in lace and other items of women's wear. I had met him only once when in June of the previous year he had come aboard the *Black Pearl* to buy a collection of French ribbons, but I knew that he held Martin Luther in high esteem, as did many of the other German merchants. I was hopeful, therefore, that he might purchase the pamphlets I had brought with me from Antwerp.

But as chance would have it, whether from lack of interest or fear of consequence, Herr Schwertzfeger was not in the market for the Luther manifesto. He did, however, give me the name of a young man who he thought might be interested.

"His name is William Tyndale," the merchant said. "I have heard him preach at Saint Dunstan-in-the-West and from what he preached I judge that he would be a likely market for any late news from the German firebrand."

Herr Schwertzfeger did show sufficient interest in the Luther manifesto to ask me what it contained.

"I know not," I said, which was the truth. Herr Schwertzfeger, as I remembered him when he had come to buy ribbons, was a tight-fisted little man who could skin you and smile and at the same time make you smile too.

Leaving the Steelyard, I walked the short distance to St. Dunstan's, where I learned from the beadle that William Tyndale would preach the following afternoon. Not being interested in preachments, I asked the beadle where Tyndale lived, thinking I might call upon him.

"Beyond the river," the beadle answered.

"A lot of country lies in that direction," I said. "Can you be a little more specific?"

"Upstream, I think. Near Ludgate."

"Ludgate's on this side of the river."

"So it is. So it is," said the beadle and gave me a long look beneath a bang of lank hair. "What is the nature of your business with Master Tyndale, if I may enquire? Nothing urgent, I trust. No? Well, you might try looking for him around Saint

Paul's. Among the bookstalls, perhaps. I've seen him there on occasion. A cloud-kisser, Master Tyndale. Always got his nose in a book. But he's most apt to be home at this time of day. He does a lot of scribbling."

Deciding that the beadle was pretty much of a dizzard and that if he knew where Tyndale lived he had no intention of telling me, I thanked him and left.

On the chance that Tyndale might be at St. Paul's, I set off in that direction.

The bookstalls at St. Paul's were mostly empty, and at the first I approached, only one person was browsing.

The clerk knew Master Tyndale by sight and for some reason took the trouble to go in search of him among the other stalls. He came back with the word that Tyndale was nowhere about but that he would be preaching, as the beadle had said, from the pulpit in St. Dunstan's on the morrow at eleven o'clock in the morning.

"Do you know by chance where he dwells?" I asked.

"Yes. In the parish of All Hallows Barking. At the residence of the cloth merchant Humphrey Monmouth."

"That lies at a considerable distance."

"Just a nice stroll for a young man of your proportions," said the bookseller, proceeding to give me a detailed account of how to find the parish.

I wondered while he was instructing me whether I should ask him if he would be interested in the Martin Luther manifesto, but in the end decided against it. A bookseller at such a prominent location as St. Paul's, I reasoned, would need to be careful of what he bought and sold.

My reasoning was wise, as the events of the morning proved.

Chapter 3

After leaving the bookstall, I had gone only the short distance to St. Paul's when I was surprised to find a large crowd gathered.

At first I thought it some sort of church celebration. Drawing nearer, however, I saw that a company of the King's troopers, attired in breastplate and cuirass as if about to leap into battle, had taken up positions near the cathedral.

Since the presence of the King's troopers usually meant trouble, I weighed the wisdom of ducking down Hillary Lane, a dark alleyway that lay at hand. But instead of fleeing I slowed my pace to a sailor's walk. I was sixteen then and less cautious in the face of danger than I am now.

At the center of the square, surrounded by a jeering crowd, were five men on seedy horses. The men rode bareback and, what was even more peculiar, awkwardly rode backward, facing the horses' tails. Around each of their necks hung a coil of rope, like a rough necklace, and attached to the rope hung books and pamphlets of various sizes. Adding to the spectacle, each man wore a tall dunce's cap made of colored paper.

I stopped as I reached the fringe of the mob. Again I weighed the wisdom of ducking into the dark alleyway. Again I gave up the idea.

Someone with a strong breath came up behind me. He was shouting at the peak of his voice, words that I had trouble understanding, being as far as I could tell a strange concoction of Welsh and Irish. Finally I made out that he was saying, "Burn the lice! Burn the lice!" He was saying it over and over.

"What lice do you refer to?" I boldly asked without turning around.

"Can't you see?" he demanded. "There before your eyes."

"I see five men riding backward with books dangling from their necks. But what does it mean? Are they maskers? Are they mimes? Are they daft?"

"Daft."

"But the lice you refer to?"

"Luther's dirty lice. Burn them all, I say."

He had been shouting in my ear, but now he moved around to stand beside me.

He proved to be a tall, thin individual in a gray, flat-brimmed hat and a gray blouse. He had a knobby, pale nose, larger than noses usually are, with nostrils that were upturned so that you could, if you wished, look directly into them. I had the feeling, as he stood there staring, that his nose was a double-barreled pistol pointed directly at me. He was the gentleman who had been dogging my uncle's footsteps, the one we had seen rowing around that morning.

"Burn them all," he repeated, casting a bilious glance upon me. "Any objections?"

"None," I said firmly. "None that I can think of."

He was carrying a walking stick as long as he was tall—in truth, it was more of a club than a stick—and I could tell by his tone that he wouldn't hesitate to use it upon me should I happen to say the wrong word.

"None," I firmly repeated. "But I don't understand why the five men ride backward."

"You don't understand, you say? Where have you been? What are you, a foreigner?"

"A sailor," I said.

"A foreign sailor, no doubt. No, you speak too glib for that. An English sailor . . ."

"Aye," I said, "but I'm away from England mostly. Hamburg, Amsterdam, Antwerp."

"Antwerp!" the tall man said, bringing his cane down hard. "Those are devilish places. But it's Wittenberg, close by, where the devil has his den."

"Wittenberg is inland," I said. "I am not familiar with it, except by name."

"The better for you," the tall man said. "Take my advice . . . "

Stopping in midsentence, he again thumped his stick upon the hard earth and again shouted, "Burn the lice!"

Now the five men were being helped from their horses and led to the center of the square. Here they were stripped of their attachments, which were then tossed into a pile, doused with oil, and lighted with a torch. Armloads of other books and pamphlets appeared at once and were thrown into the blazing pyre. The mob cheered as the flames leaped high and the smoke curled away on the cold wind.

These burnings had become quite common throughout England in the last year or so, especially around the city of London. But this was my first experience with one, and it gave me a bad start. The curses, the clenched fists, the stomping feet, the evil faces on all sides, the stench of the mob struck me as an ugly spectacle.

"You say that you're a sailor," the knob-nosed gentleman said.

"A navigator. I steer the ship."

"Of course. Sometimes you steer by the stars. Sometimes by the sun. Sometimes you steer by guess and by God. I know; I was one once myself."

This I doubted, but being in a discreet mood did not say so.

"I wonder," he went on, "if you have a place for an experienced hand. I've forgotten your ship's name. Perhaps you didn't tell me."

"*Black Pearl.*"

"A leesome name," he mused. "Where might she be located?"

"Near the Steelyard."

"Undergoing repairs?"

"No. We're loading cargo."

"I'll come by and speak to your captain," he said.

"The chances of finding a berth are slim," I said.

There was a small patch upon his chin, and he began to finger it thoughtfully. "What's your name?" he asked.

"Tom Barton."

"Mine is Belsey," he said. "Herbert Belsey."

He held out his hand and I took it, but only because it was thrust on me. Thereupon he turned away and crossed the square, moving rapidly with the heel and toe, the springing gait my uncle had once described to me.

As I watched Belsey join the crowd gathered around the burning pyre, it gave me a fine feeling of excitement to know that tucked away in my doublet were twenty pamphlets that would not burn on this day. And aboard ship, well hidden, there were two hundred more just like them.

A troop of the King's soldiers led the five men away in the direction of the Tower, whose gray bulk loomed downriver. But most of the crowd stayed on, now pressing forward to warm their hands at the smoldering fire.

Some of the King's henchmen were still loitering about the square, however. Deciding not to press my luck further, I slipped away down Jug Lane.

At the first turning I stopped and glanced back along the path I had come, half-expecting to see the tall figure of Herbert Belsey. That we had not met by accident was certain. Belsey had rowed past when we were moored at London Bridge. He had spotted our ship, had followed me to St. Paul's, and deliberately engaged me in conversation.

But for what purpose, I asked myself? And why had he dogged Uncle Jack's footsteps when we were last in London?

Chapter 4

My journey to the Monmouth residence in All Hallows Barking proved to be in vain. Master Tyndale was away, and the servant who answered my knock informed me that he was not expected before nightfall. I found him the next morning, however, at St. Dunstan-in-the-West.

I was in the church promptly at eleven, choosing a place in the back where I could duck out for a breath of fresh air should Tyndale's sermon prove dull. As a consequence, I heard little except a small passage toward the end.

"All rulers," Tyndale said, speaking slowly and quietly yet in a strong voice, "whether parents or masters, must be obeyed. At the head of all stands the king. Subjects who rise against him, rise against God. If he is cruel and downtreads them, they must bear it in patience and leave all punishment to God. Yet though kings are supreme, they may not rule as they list. They are servants of the people and must treat every man, no matter how humble, as a brother."

Master Tyndale's words—and I put them down from memory but correctly—did not encourage me. Henry VIII was violently against Martin Luther and his teachings. Therefore Tyndale, who believed that the king must be obeyed, would himself be against Luther. Therefore Tyndale would not be interested in buying the manifestoes I carried in my doublet.

It was a discouraging prospect. I even thought of leaving the church before the sermon was finished; but though the prospects were poor, I stood around until it was over and accosted Tyndale as he left the church.

William Tyndale was a young-looking man of a slender build, with a curly, sand-colored beard that hid most of his face. He had a high, bold forehead, like a promontory.

I told him that I was much taken with his preachment and introduced myself as a seaman who traveled often in Hansa waters to Hamburg and by barge as far east as Wittenberg. Since Luther lived and wrote in Wittenberg, I thought by mentioning the town that I might surprise Tyndale into making some comment that would give me a clue as to his sympathies. The ruse worked!

Master Tyndale was walking rapidly, and I am sure that in a moment, had I not mentioned Wittenberg, he would have left me behind. Upon hearing the name he instantly slowed his pace.

"In Wittenberg," he said. "Then you must have seen Martin Luther."

The tone of his voice, the reverential way he spoke the name "Martin Luther," was all the clue I needed.

"No, alas, I've never had that honor," I said. "But I do have a message from him."

Tyndale paused and waited for me to speak further, but the street was crowded with people leaving St. Dunstan's and I didn't wish to be overheard. We were opposite the Three Swans, an inn in nearby Anchor Lane, so I suggested that we repair there forthwith, to which Master Tyndale agreed.

I was not a frequenter of this place (though I had on occasion been here), preferring instead the Anchor and Chain, a lively inn close by the river. But when one was bent upon business, the Three Swans was an ideal meeting place. The clientele was mostly respectable.

Mistress Tremont, the owner's wife, greeted me at the door. She was as thin as her husband was stout, a mere wraith of a woman, scarcely discernible in the dark shadows of the inn.

"Master Tom?" she asked, examining me carefully. "You have grown since I saw you last. You must be a head taller, and filled out in the chest, too."

"Taller, it seems," I said, striking my head on a low rafter.

There was an oak serving-counter just inside the door where Master Tremont presided in a dun-colored apron. He called out a greeting, and Mistress Tremont led us into a room with three tables, very small and lit by a ship's lantern riding in brass gimbals.

Mistress Tremont brought us each something to drink and, since I had had a long, dry hour in the church, I drank my cup in a single quaff.

Master Tyndale, on the other hand, did not touch his cup until he had learned from me that indeed Luther had published a tract within the last month and that some copies of it were now in London. I did not say that I had twenty upon my person or that two hundred more were in my locker aboard ship. I still was not sure of Tyndale's sympathies.

"Have you read the tract?" he asked me.

"No," I said. As a matter of fact I could not read, not a line, but I hesitated to confess my ignorance.

Tyndale had a sharp, bodkin gaze, and he now fastened it upon me. It was plain that he could not conceive of anyone who could carry around a new Martin Luther tract and not take the time to read it.

"What is the price?" he asked.

"They are to sell for two shillings sixpence each."

"The price is high."

"So is the risk, sir."

Tyndale wore a gray woolen gown, clean but threadbare. His shoes were well worn. Obviously, he was poor. In the more than ten years that I was to know him, his shoes were always worn and his gowns always made of wool.

"Two shillings," he said.

"Two and six," I replied firmly, having no taste for a bad bargain just because of his poverty.

"What if I can help you to dispose of the lot?" he said.

"In that case, sir, I'll give you a copy gratis." I addressed him as "sir" though he appeared to be still in his early thirties, not much more than fifteen years older than I. "A special copy that carries Luther's own signature."

"I can furnish you the names of two men who deal in books," he said. "Robert Martin at Charing Cross is one. Peter Larson at Saint Paul's priory is the other. But I can't guarantee what either man will do."

"I'll see them tomorrow. Should I mention your name?"

"It is better not. You are aware that there is a severe penalty for dealing in Lutheran literature?"

"Yes," I said, remembering well the scene of yesterday—the five men degraded in the square at St. Paul's, the angry man I had talked to. "By chance do you know a gentleman who calls himself Belsey? Herbert Belsey? A tall man with a pale, turned-up nose."

"I know who he is. Why do you ask?"

"I encountered him yesterday morning at Saint Paul's. A crowd was burning books, and he was there cheering it on."

"I heard about the burning. I was going to speak about it this morning at Saint Dunstan's, but decided against it. What happened between you and Belsey?"

"I was watching the spectacle when of a sudden he came up behind me, shouting, 'Burn the lice! Burn the lice!' I asked him who the lice were, and he promptly told me."

"Disciples of the devil," Tyndale said. "Disciples of Martin Luther, the devil himself."

"Exactly; to the word," I replied. "The last time I was here—two months ago, now—Belsey followed my uncle, the ship's captain, from place to place. Who is he? Is he a spy working for the King, for Sir Thomas More, or what?"

"None and all," Tyndale said. "First off, Belsey belongs to a sect of capelclawers, a group small in numbers but fanatical. They believe that the King favors Lutheranism and so have taken upon themselves to punish those their anger fastens upon. For one thing, they make a habit of meeting ships, especially those from Germany. The spying upon your captain and upon you yourself at Saint Paul's is a common practice."

"My uncle will trim Belsey's ears one of these days," I said confidently, having first-hand knowledge of Uncle Jack's anger and strength of limb.

"It's best to leave Belsey alone. His sect has powerful ties to the Church and can do you harm. Furthermore, he's a searcher, a new one, in the employ of the Collector of Customs. I'm surprised that you haven't encountered him ere this."

Uncle Jack and I knew many searchers now and in the past, most of them by their real names, but not this Herbert Belsey. He was truly a new one to me as he would be to my uncle.

For most of two years now the Port of London had hired men to go up and down the Thames searching out all the ships that moved cargoes such as corn and wool and coins of the realm, whose export was prohibited by the King. All goods smuggled in and out of the country were subject to seizure. The owners of these cargoes, if caught and convicted, were fined, half of the fine going into the searcher's pocket. There was also a group of searchers who spied on the searchers.

"It's best to leave Belsey alone," Tyndale said. "He can do you harm."

Tyndale sat on the edge of his bench as if he intended to get up and leave at any moment, with the air of a man only half-interested in what he was saying.

I glanced about me. In the next room there was some sort of quarrel. Master Tremont was in the act of striking a drunken customer a sharp blow between the shoulder blades. There was no one in the room where we sat.

Reaching into my doublet I drew out the Luther manifestoes, slipped one out of the packet, handed it over, and put the rest back. Tyndale hid the tract away without glancing at it.

"In Wittenberg," Tyndale said, as Mistress Tremont held the door open while her husband tossed the bousy customer into Anchor Lane, "there in Wittenberg Martin Luther can work without being badgered and spied upon. That's not true in London. I've been here for most of a year and scarce a week goes by that I am not interfered with in some way by one of the numerous fanatics. Our Master Belsey is among them. I don't know whether you saw him, but he was in the congregation at Saint Dunstan's this morning."

"I didn't see him."

"He was present, nonetheless, his ears cocked to hear every sentence, searching for a word or a phrase that he might object to and report. Each time I preach he is present, or one of his group is present. There are others also, many others, who come to listen and report."

Tyndale got to his feet, leaving most of his drink untouched.

"There is nothing for me to do except leave London," he said. "I have work to do, and I cannot do it here. It can be done in Hamburg or in Wittenberg, where scholars are protected."

"We sail for Hamburg next Friday," I said. "We don't usually take passengers. They're a nuisance mostly. However . . ."

"I'll be traveling with only a light parcel of books and the clothes I stand in."

"It won't hurt to talk to my uncle," I said. "He's aboard now. Come along and talk to him. You might ship on as one of the crew. We're short three men."

"I doubt that I would make much of a sailor."

"Up to the average," I said, though, looking at his thin wrists, I had my own doubts.

As we stepped out of the tavern into Anchor Lane, a trace of sun shone overhead, but a keen southwester was blowing. A group of men stood at some distance farther up the lane. Among them I made out the lank figure, hunched against the cold, of Herbert Belsey. He was watching us as I closed the door, and as we turned toward the Thames, his gaze was still upon us.

When we reached the dock, I learned from the cook that Uncle Jack had gone ashore on urgent business, so Master Tyndale and I parted with the understanding that he would return the following night.

"Take care," Tyndale warned me. "There are many Belseys on the streets and docks of London."

Tyndale, despite the small difference in our ages, gave me a warm, fatherly look, the look that an anxious father might give a headstrong son. Since we had known each other for an hour or less, it surprised me. It was likewise embarrassing, being something that I was not accustomed to from anyone— not from my Uncle Jack or even from my own father.

I was too surprised and embarrassed to answer him.

Chapter 5

Tyndale's warning about Herbert Belsey I appreciated but did not need. It was enough to know that Belsey was a searcher hired by the Collector of Customs to spy out smuggled goods.

I lost no time, therefore, in locating Uncle Jack. I found him sitting on a bench in the Hammer and Nail, an inn he often frequented. Since he was talking religion with a sailor from King Henry's ship the *Mary Rose,* I did not interrupt him but waited until the man had taken himself off in a huff, something that usually happened when my uncle talked religion.

"Uncle Jack," I said, "I have news about Herbert Belsey."

"Belsey? Who? Tell me. Belsey? I never heard the name. Bell, Belcher, Bolton, Bedlam."

"He's the one who followed you around last time. The one we saw rowing around this morning when we moored at the bridge."

"Him?" Uncle Jack said quietly. "The one with the pale nose, eh?"

"Him!" I answered and told my uncle all that had happened at St. Paul's, of my meeting with William Tyndale at the Three Swans and how I had learned that Belsey was a searcher.

"A searcher, is he?" said Uncle Jack. "He is? Bless me, a searcher."

"Yes, and hot on our trail."

"Have no fear, nephew. Everything's in order. I have paid duties upon black copper for the arsenals, the Almadén mercury, and the six casks of Malacca cinnamon. All in order. Copper, mercury, cinnamon. Everything."

"What of the fifty lengths of Parisian silks? And the crate of three hundred oranges? And the barrel of honey? And . . . "

"Taken care of, Tom. Taken care of. Assigned this time to the Dean of Rochester. The whole lot."

The trick of false assignment had always worked for Uncle Jack. In this case, the Dean of Rochester had very special privileges. The oranges, honey, silk, and other commodities would be passed through customs without a fee. Uncle Jack, representing himself as a retainer of the Dean's, would then pick up the goods, cart them away to a nearby storehouse, and there sell them to merchants. My uncle worked on the theory that the higher on the social scale the assignee, nobleman or merchant or clergy, the safer the transaction and the more profitable.

Furthermore, Uncle Jack was a dissenter. He dissented against paying taxes—all taxes, whether to King or clergy. He was for those who were against things. He was especially enthusiastic about Martin Luther, though my uncle was not really a religious man. Having much of the pirate in him, born in a town where everyone was either a smuggler or dealt with one, he was against all authority in whatever guise he encountered it. Above all, he liked to turn a profit. It was his real religion.

"There's one more thing," I said. "Master Belsey asked me if you could hire him on as a seaman. He's coming down to talk."

"Coming to the ship? Here? This requires mountainous gall, eh?"

"That's what he said."

"Think you he's serious?"

"Appears to be."

"When does he come?"

"Sometime today, is my guess."

Uncle Jack got to his feet. "Then," he said, "we should leave and hurry along for fear of missing him. Hurry, eh?"

"You haven't forgotten so soon what Tyndale told me about Belsey?" I said as we set off for the ship. "We'll have a searcher aboard."

"If he's like the other searchers, we can do more business with him than without him. Business."

This was a puzzling remark, and I did not take it seriously. On the contrary, when we reached the ship, I immediately set about removing Luther's pamphlets from the hold.

The two hundred copies were hidden away in a shipment of French silks. I had wrapped them tightly in a scarf ere we left the port of Antwerp and secreted this package in the center of one of the bales, where it could not be discovered except the bale were opened and the silk taken out length by length. Customs had passed the shipment without so much as a glance, and had given me a docket in proof of ownership.

I thought first of hiring a carter to deliver the bale, but gave up the idea when I realized that the silk would need to be returned once the pamphlets were removed, for it was the more valuable of the two. The package was of a goodly size, yet I managed to hide it under my greatcoat.

Following Master Tyndale's advice, I went to see Robert Martin, the bookseller located in Charing Cross, and after an hour or more of friendly haggling said, "Take it or want it." Whereupon he took it.

Throughout the journey, coming and going, I watched for Herbert Belsey. I failed to see him among the throng that crowded this busy part of London, but I had a strong suspicion that he was somewhere close at hand.

In that, I was wrong. When I returned to the ship, I found him aboard; he and Uncle Jack were standing at the door of the roundhouse talking quite amiably, like old acquaintances.

Master Belsey did not recognize me as the young man he had spoken to before—at least he said nothing to me as I passed him on my way below.

After I reached the lower deck, I paused at the foot of the companionway and through the open scuttle above, listened to him speaking.

"A day or two ago I followed in your lee for most of an hour," he said to my uncle, "trying to get up the nerve to approach you."

"I failed to notice," Uncle Jack replied.

"You have a rather forbidding manner, if I may be so bold," Belsey said, talking in a much softer voice than he had used on me at St. Paul's. "You have the bold presence of a commander of the King's fleet. A presence that does not invite familiarity, I must say."

It was true that we were in need of seamen. As a result of the storm off Gottenburg, three of the crew had deserted upon reaching London. Still, I was surprised to hear my uncle say, "I can put you to use forthwith. Your qualifications?"

"Five years on my last ship, during which there were two voyages to the Indies."

Someone was tapping his boot against the deck. It sounded like a noise Uncle Jack would make.

"Come aboard before tomorrow eve," my uncle said. "We leave for Deptford to repair some nifling damage to our rig. Nifling."

As I listened, there was other conversation, which the noise of a passing ship drowned out; then I heard the captain's steps cross the deck overhead, and a moment later his boots appeared on the top rung of the companionway. Deciding not to hide the fact that I had overheard his conversation, I stood my ground and spoke as soon as he reached the deck.

"Why, sir, did you hire Herbert Belsey?" I asked.

Ordinarily I did not speak to my uncle in this manner, for the sound reason that he would most surely have boxed my ears. But for a reason that will appear later, he did not take offense at my boldness.

He stood at the foot of the companionway, looking at me from his great height. "We are in dire need of men," he said.

"Not so dire as that," I answered. "We'll have a snooping spy aboard, nosing around, snooping into everything we do."

Uncle Jack brushed his beard with the back of his hand. Gazing down at me, his eyes in the light that came from the companionway were sea blue and cold, cold as the sea.

"We need him for the rigging," he said.

"But then, afterward we'll have him underfoot for the voyage," I replied. "He cannot get off the ship and walk away, once we are at sea."

"Perhaps we'll give him a chance to try. A chance, eh?"

With these words my uncle smiled. His lips showed red against his beard. He looked down at me in a kindly fashion, as much as to say, "You are, Tom Barton, quite close of kin, verily my dear nephew, the son of my dear brother, yet withal you are somewhat of an airling."

He then walked away, leaving me to ponder his strange words.

Chapter 6

The rest of the day I spent at the Steelyard, banking the money made on the sale of the pamphlets, then investing it in sixty lengths of English woolen. Woolen goods brought an excellent price in Hamburg and even better prices on the Rhine, at Dusseldorf, Cologne, and beyond.

In the three and a half years of service with my uncle, first as a cabin boy and roustabout, now as coxswain-navigator, I had saved enough of my modest wages and made enough on my simple transactions along the Rhine and the countries of the Lowlands and in London to think about seafaring on my own.

For the past year I had been hopeful that my uncle would offer to take me in as a partner—not a full partner perhaps, but as a half partner or even as a third partner. I gave out many hints toward this end, but to no avail. Finally, I screwed up my courage and broached the subject directly.

"I've been working with you now for most of four years," I said, "at a small wage. Much smaller, Uncle, than I could get should I work for someone else."

"You have working for me rare privileges that you would not have elsewhere," my uncle replied.

"I don't want privileges," I said. "I want rights and shares. I wish to be a partner. I am prepared to give you fifty pounds and sign an agreement for the same amount within two years."

We were standing in the peak of the ship, side by side, looking out at the sea. My uncle turned and looked at me as if he had never seen me before, as if I had grown two heads. He had difficulty speaking.

"Remember, nephew, that you are my only heir," he sputtered. "One day, and it may well come soon, the *Black Pearl* will be yours. You'll be captain and sole owner of a fine ship."

Since my uncle was only nine years older than I and of a sturdier constitution by far, the prospects of my inheriting the ship were dim indeed.

Aware of my prospects, seeing the state he was in at the mere mention of a partnership, I let the matter drop. But I still kept fresh the dream of being captain of my own ship.

Down the Thames at the port of Deptford lay a flotilla of old hulls—ships that had sailed on the Indies run and for one reason or another had been laid up. Of these hulls one in particular had caught my fancy. Her name was *Star of India.* Once when I pointed her out to my uncle, he had said scornfully that she reminded him of a "sea-going cow."

On the morrow, in spite of my uncle's contemptuous remark, I planned to take another look at the *Star of India.* Her price was more than I held, by considerable. But her owner, a retired merchantman, had agreed to take a third of the asking price as a down payment and allow me five years to pay the balance. Once I had enough for the down payment, the rest would be easy, for there was a good profit in trading English merchandise through the Rhine country and, in return, Rhine merchandise in London.

The problem was how to accumulate the money for a first payment. As matters now stood, I lacked the sum of sixty pounds, or about the amount I could hope to accumulate in the next two years both from wages and the profits from trading. In addition, that much or more would be required to put the *Star of India* into shape.

There was no chance that my uncle would have a change of heart. He was not an ungenerous man and, as I was his only kin on earth, he had a certain affection for me, but the *Black Pearl* was his love, his wife and child.

Yes, unfortunately, this road was closed to me and, should I fail to gather sufficient capital to buy the *Star of India* or a hull of similar dimensions, there was still the chance of joining the House of Jacob Fugger as a coxswain, perhaps a captain of one of its countless ships.

I had always admired Jacob Fugger. His life was an inspiration to me. At the age of fourteen he had been a successful merchant, and now he was the head of the greatest banking house in the world.

Jacob Fugger loaned money to popes and kings and financed wars in many places—wherever anyone wished to fight a war.

He had paid half the cost of the scheme that had made Charles V Emperor of half the world, the Holy Roman Empire. He had even loaned chests of gold to our own King, Henry VIII.

Now that my uncle had enlisted the services of Master Belsey, whose presence would curtail my profits somewhat, it was time for me to come to a decision—either to make a great effort to purchase one of the hulls at Deptford or to seek employment with the House of Jacob Fugger.

Whether Tyndale came on as a member of the crew or solely as a passenger to Hamburg, he might put me in the way of material in this northern city that would profit me to bring back to England. Hamburg was near Wittenberg, the town where Luther lived, preached, and wrote his manifestoes. Therefore, with Tyndale's advice, I should be able to find a goodly stock of Lutheran material, much more than I had been able to collect in Antwerp.

In any event, the decision to buy a Deptford hull or, failing that, to seek employment with Jacob Fugger must be made upon my return from Hamburg, and no later than early summer.

Chapter 7

Master Tyndale came aboard that evening shortly after supper.

I had already spoken to my uncle and told him that Tyndale wished passage to Hamburg. I had spoken in a most persuasive tone, emboldened by the knowledge that Tyndale, once in Hamburg, could greatly help by putting me in touch with Luther's printings.

My purchase of the *Star of India* depended, I told myself, upon transporting Master Tyndale to Hamburg.

But nothing I had said could change Uncle Jack's rule against permitting passengers aboard his ship, even so few as one. I shifted then to the possibility of hiring Tyndale as a member of the crew. This also failed. It was not until I mentioned that Tyndale was a preacher, that in fact I had heard him preach at St. Dunstan's, and that, moreover, he was a staunch follower of the German firebrand, that my uncle showed any interest.

I sent a messenger for Tyndale forthwith, and two hours later he came alongside in a hired wherry.

Fearing that if I called my uncle he would appear on deck in a sulky mood, the two men would then shout at each other over the distance of half a ship's length, and the meeting would end in failure, I let down our rope ladder and, without calling my uncle, beckoned the man aboard.

I was pleased that I had not called my uncle on deck, for Tyndale missed the first rung, doused one foot in the river, and came up crablike and out of breath, in a landlubberly manner that would have made Uncle Jack laugh.

I led him off to my uncle's cabin where, the day being chill, there was a peat fire burning in the small grate.

The two men were a startling contrast to the eye. My uncle had to stoop to keep from bumping his head on the carlings, and had an enormous black beard attached to a great bald, shining head. The other was so short, so thin, so small of bone and marrow that well he could have been made from the spare pieces left over from the fashioning of Uncle Jack.

It was my intent to remain with the two of them in the cabin, to steer the conversation along the right path should it falter, but without ceremony or apology my uncle closed the door in my face. Hoping to overhear a word or two, I hung about and after a while did hear my uncle shout, "The answer for such mouths is a fist that brings blood to the nose," and, in a quieter tone, Tyndale reply, "That sounds like Martin Luther." "It is such," answered my Uncle Jack.

Thereafter I heard nothing more, since I had to leave my post and go forward to see to the lanterns, which someone had forgotten to light. As I was returning to the cabin, Tyndale emerged and, without a word or glance in my direction, descended the ladder in his crablike fashion and was rowed away. With sinking heart I watched him go, certain that my plans had failed.

I felt a heavy but friendly hand upon my shoulder. "He'll be coming back," Uncle Jack said. "He'll be traveling with us. Praise the Lord."

"Hoorah!" I exclaimed, watching the wherry disappear into the night. "Hoorah for Hamburg!"

My Uncle Jack said, "A boisterous young man, this Master Tyndale. Learned in many languages—Hebrew and Greek and Latin, German, French and Spanish, and Italian and more perchance. I swear I've never heard of such before. He's translating the Bible, the New Testament. But he can't finish the work here nor bring it to publication because of Henry's laws. Where he's going, they're of the Lutheran faith. He'll be safe there. Praise the Lord."

"He'll print Bibles in English?" I said, scarcely trusting my ears.

"Bibles in the King's English. Bibles for England!" Uncle Jack said. "Think on it, eh?"

Three of the crew had come up and were standing now against the rail, within earshot, their eyes on the disappearing wherry.

Uncle Jack gave me a nudge, and I followed him into the roundhouse. The peat fire was smoking badly, so he left the door ajar. We stood peering at each other through the smoke.

"Tyndale plans to make a printing of five thousand copies of his translation," he said, lowering his voice.

"Five thousand?" I exclaimed, visions of Bibles by the shipload, money by the barrel, exploding in my brain.

"I have agreed to see that the Bibles get to England," he said. "We'll bring them here as fast as ever they're printed. I haven't worked on just how, but we'll get them here. To London, eh?"

"It's against the King's law," I reminded him. "We can swing for it."

"Not you, nephew, not you."

"But I want to share the work and the dangers." Pausing, I added, "And the profits, too, Uncle Jack. We'll make . . ."

"Not so much as you might think, nephew."

But I could tell by the glint in his eyes that he was planning upon a handsome profit. Why else would he undertake such a hazardous scheme?

I was puzzled. With all the costs of printing the books and our profits added to that, how could Tyndale ever make enough to pay him for his trouble?

Uncle Jack stooped, picked up the poker, and stirred the fire. Then he thrust the poker toward me as if to emphasize his words.

"Master Tyndale risks his life so that all England can read the Bible," he said. "Now there are few who can because they cannot read Latin, in which the Bible is printed. I recall what Tyndale said as he left these quarters. These are his own words: 'I want to translate the Bible into English so that every plowboy can read it.' Every plowboy, mind you. And even you, Master Tom Barton, can then read it. Once you learn to read, eh?"

My father and mother were God-fearing people who died of the plague in the bad summer of 1520. Thereafter I left home and went to sea, and perforce was influenced more by the ways of the world than by their devout beliefs. My uncle's influence, during the four years of my service on his ship, had tended to discourage me in religious matters. And in my education, as well.

Uncle Jack still had the hot poker pointed at me.

"I'll read the Bible that Master Tyndale translates," I said.

"And ponder it."

"And ponder it," I agreed.

"Praise the Lord," said Uncle Jack.

But there was a hollow sound to his words. I had heard it oft before. It came when he said, in his deepest voice, "Praise the Lord." He was not, I was certain, as interested in my pondering the Bible as he was in the tidy profit the books would bring.

Chapter 8

Master Tyndale arrived early the next morning with a parcel of books in a string bag and the shabby clothes he stood up in. I found him a berth in the forecastle, a dark cubbyhole where we kept spare anchor chain.

No sooner had he stowed his books and lighted a candle than he had pen and paper out and had sat himself down to write on a barrel head. We moved the ship downriver to Deptford and docked her there in the yard, and on he wrote. He was still writing when I went to call him for supper.

Master Belsey came aboard at Deptford, carrying a small trunk on his back, a sailor's trunk that looked as if it had been around the world many times. I found him a bunk in the stern amid the cargo, as far from Tyndale as possible, and promptly put him to work cleaning out the bilge. It was a dirty job, but to my surprise he went about it with a right good will.

I did not look forward to supper, since we had only one mess, everyone, captain, coxswain, and crew, all eating at one table. Uncle Jack liked this arrangement because it gave him a chance to talk three times a day to an audience that could not escape.

But supper went well. Tyndale sat apart from Belsey, and if the two spoke, I failed to hear it. Afterward, while the crew sat about chatting, Tyndale rose quietly and left. As Uncle Jack and I made a last round of the ship before bed, he accosted us on deck and asked for another candle. My uncle gave him two and promised him a handful before we sailed.

Our cargo of woolens stored, the mast repaired, and supplies stowed, we caught the first of the ebb two days later and coasted downriver at a leesome rate. We lost half a day at the river's mouth with a blinding fog, then a whole day at Gravesend with the rumor of a pirate scare in the harbor.

The previous day a merchantman had been boarded and scuttled a few leagues to the northeast, and all but one of its crew killed. There were nine ships waiting at anchor to make the Channel crossing when we arrived.

Fortunately for all, the *Mary Rose,* the King's man-of-war, sailed by chance down from Portsmouth under full canvas on her way to Ostend. She came about after sighting us, and after an exchange of information we were told to fall in astern, which we gratefully did.

It was a pretty sight to see—the *Mary Rose* keening along forward of us, even though she was sailing with half her canvas so that we slower ships could keep apace. From her masts the great high-castled carrack floated long streamers of Tudor green and white, the red-crossed flag of St. George, and above all the royal standard.

A league or so off the coast of Cornwall, she opened her gun ports on the starboard side and fired five shots, *duf, duf, duf, duf, duf.* Whether she was firing at a pirate ship we did not know, only that we were not attacked then or later.

The mighty ship led us for the better part of the morning; then raising all sails, she left us to continue the crossing alone.

"She carries near two hundred big guns of brass and iron," Uncle Jack said.

We were standing forward, the two of us, with a fine view of the brilliantly painted ship as she pulled away on the calm sea under a sky of slow, white clouds.

"And her racks are stacked with a thousand long bows, swords, and pikes," he went on. "She's filled with armored men. They even cling to the fighting tops like nests of ants. At any moment she can launch forth a veritable blizzard of shot and shell and a flood of fighting soldiers. Yet, yet the *Mary Rose,* and the *Great Harry,* and all the rest of the King's conquering ships cannot withstand that which Master Tyndale now prepares there below in his darksome cubby. In that fusty hole the true words of the Lord, shining forth from the Testament, shall sweep all England before them. The true words. Praise the Lord."

Despite the "Praise the Lord," I think that perhaps, for the first time in his life, Uncle Jack really believed what he had intoned.

"He works diligently," I said. "He has about used up all our candles."

"Fire him a lantern," said Uncle Jack.

"We're very short on lanterns."

"Take him a lantern."

At dusk I complied with my uncle's request against my better judgment, robbing one of our set of riding lights. As I reached the passageway on my way to Tyndale, I saw standing before the door of his cubby a tall figure I recognized at once as Master Belsey.

Shining the lantern in his face, I asked him if he was looking for somebody.

"I'm looking for Master Tyndale," he said. "He was absent from the noon mess. I thought he might be seasick, inasmuch as we've been in a roll-and-pitch most of the day."

"We'll see," I said.

Believing not a word of Belsey's story, I knocked on the door. There was no answer, and only after I had knocked a second and a third time did Tyndale appear.

He wore a cap, but his hair stuck out as if he had been worrying it. There were books everywhere—on the cubby floor, on the barrel head, on a shelf against the ship's bulkhead. Papers lay about in a great disorder.

"I've brought you a light at the captain's request," I said, passing the lantern to him. "Tomorrow I'll bring you a jug of oil to replenish it."

He thanked me absent-mindedly and turned back to his papers. Belsey took a step forward as if bent upon entering the cubby, but I blocked his path. Closing the door firmly, more or less in his face, I waited for him to shuffle off down the passage.

Tyndale called to me, and I went back inside the cubbyhole, tripping over a stack of books, and closed the door.

"Have you read the Luther manifesto yet?" he asked, not looking away from the paper he was writing on.

"No, sir, I haven't."

He looked up from his paper, looked me squarely in the face.

"Can you read, Master Barton?" he asked.

I didn't intend to be truthful, but he kept looking at me until, in desperation, at last I blurted out, "No, I can't. I've never read a word in my life. Only the letters on a compass card. *N* and *S* and *E* and *W.* That's all I've ever read."

"Do you want to learn to read?"

"Yes," I said, "but not tonight. Tonight I have things I have to do."

"Then tomorrow," Tyndale said, "we'll begin. Tomorrow morning early."

Master Tyndale started upon me at dawn. As soon as breakfast was over, he marched me into his cubbyhole, like a true professor, and sat me down on a pile of books. I thought of several duties that I needed to perform in other parts of the ship. I hoped that it would blow up a storm and he would become seasick. But all my excuses came to naught, and the weather stayed fair.

He used part of the New Testament on me, the one he was translating into English. First he showed me a Bible written in Greek and a Bible written in Hebrew and one written in German and one in French and then one written in Latin.

"Why do you need a Bible written in English?" I asked him, "when already you have so many Bibles?"

"Because Englishmen read the English language and do not read other languages," he said.

"But, sir, you have to be able to read English words before you can read an English Bible."

"Yes, that's why we're here, so that you may learn to read English words. To know English words when you see them, and then be able to speak them, and then to know what the words you have spoken mean."

"It sounds very difficult," I said.

"It is."

Far off above my head I heard the slatting of our mainsail, which needed trimming at once, and I spoke of this to Master Tyndale.

"I'll go and see that it is trimmed," I said. "And then I'll come back."

"Someone else will trim the sail. There are others in the crew who can do that. Stay where you are, and we'll begin our first lesson."

I slid off the stack of books, which were uncomfortable, and sat on the floor.

"We'll start at a part of the Bible called The First Epistle of Paul the Apostle to the Corinthians. Later I will tell you about Paul and who the Corinthians were. Now we'll start with Paul's words and discuss how these words sounded as he spoke them to the people who had gathered to hear them.

Though I spake with tongues of men and angels, and yet had no love, I were even as sounding brass: or as a tinkling cymbal. And though I could prophesy, and understood all secrets, and all knowledge: yee, if I had all faith so that I could move mountains out of their places, and yet had no love, I were nothing.

I listened, though still hearing the slat of the mainsail. There was a sweet, strong sound as he spoke the words. They filled the cubbyhole with their music.

"Now come, Tom, and stand here."

His manuscript lay open on a slanting bench we once used for anchor chain. Master Tyndale pointed to the first letter of the first word he had read.

"This is the letter *T*," he said. "What does it look like to you?"

Nothing came to mind.

"Does it look like a stick? A stick with a hat on it?"

I looked again over his shoulder, at his finger pointing out the letter *T*, and suddenly saw that it did look like a stick with a hat atop.

"Yes, I see it now," I said.

"Well, when you see it again, you'll recognize it as the letter *T*."

"I will, sir. But how many letters are there altogether?"

"Twenty-six."

I gasped but said nothing. Twenty-six!

"Now pronounce the letter."

Like a child, I said, "*T*."

"Now the first letter of the third word," Master Tyndale said, pointing at an *S*. "What does that look like to you?"

"To me," I said, of a sudden inspired, "it looks like a snake."

"Exactly," Master Tyndale said. "And now what sort of sound is made by a snake?"

"It hisses."

"So does the letter *S*. Speak it and see."

I did and I sounded like a snake hissing.

"We'll have another lesson soon in the English Bible," Tyndale said, "the way it should be read. The Greek tongue is much closer to English than it is to Latin. It has more grace and sweetness and pure understanding. And the qualities of the Hebrew tongue agree a thousand times more with English than with Latin. English boys speak English words. Why then should they not read the Bible in English?"

Above me I heard Uncle Jack calling my name. Master Tyndale heard it, too, and put away his manuscript and gave me a pat on the back, which felt odd because it was the first pat I'd had in a long time.

Chapter 9

A small southwester was blowing as we approached the first of the Frisian Islands. We therefore changed our course, took the more protected, landward passage, slipped by Wangerooge on a cloudy morning, and reached the Hamburg estuary at nightfall.

A light but steady rain had begun to fall by the time we had our anchor set.

It was therefore a surprise to Uncle Jack and me that Tyndale insisted upon leaving the ship. He had no friends in Hamburg and in fact had never been in the port before. We tried to prevail upon him to wait until morning when the weather might improve and he could at least see his way around.

But we failed in our efforts, so I helped him to gather together his books, his writing materials, and few oddments.

The sky was dark with rushing clouds as we pushed away into the broad estuary, crowded with ships whose riding lights cast a great shine upon the water. The tide being at neither ebb nor flood, I had some difficulty bringing the boat to the landing, a sandspit that ran out from the river mouth, on which were two shipbuilding yards and a roisterous inn.

Uncle Jack was not in good humor, therefore, when I did make shore. As Tyndale picked up his bag and looked as if he might go striding off into the dark and the rain, my uncle grabbed the bag in one hand, Tyndale by the arm in the other, and forthwith launched us all into the inn.

The River Queen, filled with gixies, fustylugs, and sailors, was not a place suited to serious discussion, and I doubt that in all its lurid history the Bible had ever been mentioned. But if never again, it was mentioned that evening.

Uncle Jack ordered bowls of oyster stew for each of us and, since Tyndale still looked as if he might go striding off into the darkness at any moment, immediately brought up the subject of the Bible.

"When, Master Tyndale, can we expect them?" Uncle Jack asked. "Soon, eh?"

"I'm going now to Wittenberg where Martin Luther is and where I'll have a chance to talk to him and to perfect, at least to improve, my knowledge of Greek there at the university. When my translation is finished, I'll go to Cologne, there being no good presses in Wittenberg. Two fine presses are located in Cologne. Furthermore, Cologne is on the Rhine, near the book market and its great book fair."

"Cologne is not far distant from England," Uncle Jack said. "It's more convenient than any city except Antwerp. Close by, eh?"

"I may go to Antwerp later. It will be a good idea to have two printings going on at once," Tyndale said.

"But you haven't told us yet when we can expect the first," Uncle Jack said, trying to conceal his impatience. "The first. The first."

"Not soon."

"When? In two months? In three months, eh?"

"Not before next spring. By then, I hope."

"In what numbers? Two thousand? Three?"

"Five thousand."

"We have a big hold. We can handle thrice that number," said Uncle Jack, bragging. "Five thousand."

"But I may be unable to find the money to pay for even one small printing."

Uncle Jack spooned his thick oyster stew in silence, thinking hard. To carry Bibles that someone else had printed, Bibles that were already paid for, was one thing. To put up money of his own for a printing, with all its hazards of failure and detection, was quite another.

He thought hard for a long time, finished his stew, ordered a second bowl, and said, "I'll return to you, Master Tyndale, all profits I make on the sale of your New Testament in England. All profits, after our expenses. Expenses are heavy, eh, Tom? Heavy, eh?"

"That's a generous offer," Tyndale said.

It was clear to me, and surely to Uncle Jack, that Tyndale was interested only in having his Bible printed and distributed in England. His last thought was of any profit he might make for himself.

"Upon my word the offer stands," my uncle said. "We'll carry your Bibles to England, from Cologne or Antwerp. It doesn't matter which, does it, Tom? We'll sell them there, deduct our expenses, and send you the rest. A fine deal, eh?"

Tyndale growing impatient to be on his way, we parted soon with a round of warm farewells.

The River Queen had places to sleep, but it was a noisy inn, where if you were not robbed or relieved of your life, it would be a true miracle. We therefore advised him to return to the ship—we would send him off bright and early—but, as before, he strongly leaned toward the road and we let him go.

I felt a twinge of regret as he walked off in the rain.

At first, on the day he had stumbled aboard the ship in true landlubberly fashion, I was prone to laugh. But seeing him at his writing all day and far into the night, asking for nothing except a handful of candles, I had come to think of him in a different way.

Furthermore, there was the debt I owed him for his trying to teach me to read. He had given me three lessons on our way to Hamburg, three long, hard lessons. I hadn't learned much, but I had made a start; at least he said that I had.

There was something else I felt too. It was more than regret at his going. It was more than thanks for what he had done to help me learn to read. He had become a part of my life. I would miss him and his counseling words.

"What will I do about my reading?" I shouted.

Tyndale stopped and turned around. "You'll find some papers I left in your bunk. You'll be able to read them. If not, keep at it until you do."

He disappeared into the rain.

Uncle Jack said, "What's this reading business, eh?"

"Master Tyndale has taught me to read."

My uncle grunted. "It takes years to learn reading. Years."

He had gone to school and could read both Latin and English. It didn't seem to please him that I was learning to read.

"A waste of time, boy. A waste. One reader in the family's enough," he said as we lowered our heads against the driving rain. "It will get you into trouble, Tom, boy. Trouble. Let me do the reading, and you tend to the ship, eh?"

Chapter 10

Before nightfall of the next day, we had unloaded our Hamburg cargo. My woolens brought the profits I had hoped for, and with them I invested in a bale of northern furs, for which there was always a good market in London.

We had begun to take in the anchor, when Uncle Jack spied Belsey at the rail. Huddled in a greatcoat, his leather trunk on his shoulder, he was talking to someone in the skiff that lay alongside.

"What ho?" Uncle Jack called down. "What?"

Belsey did not answer, and my uncle called a second time. Belsey then said, not looking up, but keeping his eyes all the while on the boatman, "We're going ashore."

"Ashore?" Uncle Jack shouted, starting toward the ladder that led to the lower deck. "We still have cargo to unload in Antwerp."

Uncle Jack went down the ladder and walked over to where Belsey was standing.

"I made no contract for Antwerp," Belsey said. "Hamburg's my destination."

"We're sailing for Antwerp within an hour," Uncle Jack said. "And you sail with us."

My uncle nodded to me, then leaned over the rail and told the boatman to secure the hooks and prepare to hoist.

On my way to the lower deck, sensing trouble unless I mustered help, I motioned to two men lounging at the forepeak. They came at a run. I turned back, and suddenly there were four of us facing Belsey. Although Belsey was more agile than at first he had looked, he must have realized that he was outnumbered, for he sullenly backed off and disappeared down a forward hatch, taking trunk and bag with him.

The tide was right as we dropped downstream before dark had settled, and we caught a fresh wind before we sighted Wrangroot.

Supper was on time, and since the pork was half-done and swimming in yellow grease, it meant that Stilton the sailmaker was in the galley. As for Belsey, he took his place at the table, ate at length in his customary fashion, and acted as if nothing had happened. He even paused eating long enough to ask a question of Uncle Jack, who was in the midst of one of his nightly discourses.

But the truce between us did not last.

The following noon the brisk wind that had driven us south died away. Suddenly we found ourselves becalmed on a mirrorlike sea. Then as we rode there with limp sails for an hour or more, not knowing what to expect—whether to take in canvas or not—a bank of wet fog crept down upon us.

The fog came from eastward, from the land, which I estimated to be at a distance of some twenty miles. Ships— and we were in a lane where they might be expected—could sail by without ever taking heed of what took place aboard the *Black Pearl*. And those of us on board passed within a few paces of each other without recognition.

The weather was perfect for the plan Belsey had devised and quietly set afoot.

I was the first to suffer. The sun shone weakly overhead and the fog was at its thickest when, having finished the noon meal, I carried my knife and empty bowl into the galley. The galley ran crosswise of the ship, from beam to beam, with a narrow door to starboard. I had no sooner put my foot over the threshold of this door than I was seized from either side and at once hit a resounding blow upon the head. The blow might well have rendered me unconscious, as was the intent I am sure of whoever delivered it, but by good fortune it only dazed me.

Instinct and anger tempted me to fight back, but I was securely held by two assailants whom I could not see through the fog and galley smoke. Then something told me to pretend that I had been injured more severely than I was.

With this thought, I thereupon went limp in the grasp of the two men who held me—one of whom I recognized, by the whistling sound I had often heard him make in the past, to be Stilton, the sailmaker. I was allowed to fall upon the floor and was given a purposeful kick in the stomach. One side of my face lay against the hot bricks of the stove, but I dared not move lest they think me in possession of my senses.

Far off and then much nearer I heard the deep-toned bells of passing ships. The sound of the warning bells faded away. It was quiet in the galley, and all I could hear was the sound of John Stilton's breathing.

On a sudden there were whispered commands; then someone knelt above me—I judged it to be neither Stilton nor Belsey— and began to tie my wrists with a length of rope that reeked with the smell of tar.

Opening my eyes fully, I took good aim and kicked out with both feet. The blow caught my assailant—whom I now saw was really Stilton—square in the midriff. He gave out a low grunt, then a wavering moan, and fell headlong against the forward bulwark.

Jumping to my feet, I paused long enough to snatch up a long piece of oak stovewood, which I laid upon Stilton's bald head, and in two long strides I reached the deck.

The fog seemed to have thinned somewhat; I now made out the dim outlines of two figures struggling at the rail, some twenty paces from where I stood. The two uttered not a word nor cry, either one of them, but there was the sound of straining bodies and shifting feet.

Then there was a sudden outburst of oaths, which I recognized to have come from my Uncle Jack. With the oak cudgel in my hand, I ran forward, not knowing who his assailant was, though I strongly suspected it to be Belsey.

When I reached the two men, before I had a chance to swing the cudgel in defense of my uncle, he broke the other's hold upon his neck. He then stooped and in a final burst of strength shoved him across the rail. As the man reached out to save himself, I saw that it was Belsey.

He fell without a sound, his arms stretched backward, into the sea. Then he was lost to sight in the fog and the gray rolling waves.

With flapping sails, slowly with the current, the ship moved on.

My uncle, who only a moment before had been standing solidly in front of me, I now found lying prone upon the deck, his head turned to one side and blood coming from his mouth. I gave out a desperate cry for help, not knowing whom my cry would bring. To my great relief, Ed Groat came running, and together we carried Uncle Jack to his quarters and laid him there upon his bunk.

John Stilton had some skills as a surgeon, but we could not expect help from him. I therefore ordered water to be heated and, when it came, bathed my uncle's wounds and ministered to him as best I could.

He lay upon his bunk, saying nothing, for that night and most of the morning of the next day. We bled him twice during that time, but it did not help. Near to noon, with the fog gone, the sun out again, and a wind in the sails, Uncle Jack opened his eyes, which had been closed all the time, looked at me, and said, "I'll be on deck tomorrow. On deck. Praise the Lord."

And at noon on the morrow he was there, standing on his two good legs.

BOOK TWO

Chapter 11

The following summer—this was the momentous year of 1525—we kept the pact we had made with William Tyndale on that night just twelve months before as we stood in the rain at the door of the River Queen.

We kept the pact only because Uncle Jack had been a party to it. Because his greed had overcome his caution, we came to Cologne. Nothing else in this world could have brought us there at that dangerous time, for the town and countryside roundabout were rife with murders and beheadings.

We had heard rumors before we sailed from London that all of the southern German states were in revolt. This seemed fanciful to me and also to others more knowledgeable than I, but upon arriving in Antwerp I found the rumors to be much milder than the truth. Europe, indeed, was aflame from the Alps to the middle reaches of the Rhine.

In the year since I had last seen William Tyndale, using the papers he had left for me, I had learned to read English. I could not read it well, but if I took my time I could understand most of what I read. I would have learned to read better had not Uncle Jack put obstacles in my way, ordering me to do unnecessary work when he knew I wished to study.

With my new knowledge I spent several hours each day in the office of Jacob Fugger. The company had offices throughout Europe and from them came daily reports of political and business events. Some of the information was confidential and meant only for their own use, but much of it they offered freely to merchants and shipmasters.

It was clear from their reports that the trouble along the Rhine was caused by a revolt of the peasants against the lords of the realm. I was aware that, for a number of years, Martin Luther had encouraged them to rebel against their oppressors.

In the Fugger offices one morning, I read Luther's latest pamphlet, printed less than a week earlier:

> We have no one on earth to thank for this mischievous rebellion except you, princes and lords, and especially you,

blind bishops whose hearts are hardened against the Holy Gospel . . . You do nothing but flog and rob your subjects in order that you may lead a life of splendor and pride . . . The peasants are mustering, and this must result in the ruin, destruction and desolation of Germany by cruel murder and bloodshed, unless God shall be moved by our repentance to prevent it.

A dispatch brought in by courier the previous day from Mainz, not far distant upriver from Cologne, told how Archbishop Albrecht had fled the city in fear of his life.

Another dispatch came from Weinsberg, describing how rebel peasants had besieged the town, whose overlord, Count Ludwig von Helfenstein, was widely hated for his cruelties.

A group of peasants asked for a meeting to discuss their grievances. Whereupon the Count and his cohorts rode out and cut them to pieces. A few days later the rebels broke through the walls and killed forty of the Count's men-at-arms. The Count, his wife, and sixteen knights were taken prisoner. The seventeen men were ordered to run the gauntlet of rebels armed with swords, daggers, and pikes while the Count's wife was compelled to look on.

As the Count walked the gauntlet to his death beneath the blows of a hundred weapons, peasants called upon him to remember his own brutalities.

"You wrung the last penny out of us," one man shouted.

Another cried, "Your horses, dogs, and huntsmen have trodden down my crops."

A third man cried, "You thrust my brother into a dungeon because he did not bow his head as you passed by."

A fourth cried, "You caused the hands of my father to be cut off because he killed a hare in his own field."

Dispatches of a similar kind I read every morning for days, and at the end Uncle Jack and I debated with ourselves for most of a week whether to engage passage up the Rhine to Cologne in an attempt to seek out Tyndale.

Many things weighed against the idea. For one thing, there was no assurance that once in Cologne we would find him, or that he had completed his translation of the Bible and had found someone to print it. Aside from these objections, there was the very real danger of our becoming embroiled in some fatal happening.

Above all, the pact called upon us to return to Tyndale the profits we made from the sale of his Bible. The profits were large, but we were not called upon to deliver them at the risk of the ship and our lives. Tyndale could wait.

And yet, against caution and common sense, and having weighed everything in the balance, we decided to go in search of one man among the many thousands in the great city of Cologne, not knowing that we should find him, or, if we did, that he would have finished his printing of the Bible.

At the last moment, after he had paid for our passage on a river barge, Uncle Jack decided that we could not afford to keep the ship idle in port while we both went to Cologne. He therefore took on a cargo for Portugal, and sent me off up the Rhine on my own.

"Keep me informed," he said. "Send word to me in care of the English Merchant Adventurers. When you find Tyndale, let me know. And when the Bibles will be ready. Let me know, Tom. I'll moor the *Black Pearl* and be there by the first barge that sails. The first barge. Eh?"

Chapter 12

Fighting a brisk current, I moored near Cologne on a cloudless day.

From a farmer I bargained for a horse and, astride it, set off early in the morning for Cologne, taking the road that followed close upon the river. It was a warm day, the road was in fine repair, and, though the horse was more used to drawing a cart, well before noon the great cathedral rose before me.

Upon entering the city, I stopped at the first inn I came to. It was crowded with farmers, all of whom seemed to be talking at once, in a dialect that I did not understand. I caught the name of Martin Luther several times and the name of Archbishop Albrecht, but learned no more than that everyone was concerned about the revolt.

I rode on and nearer the heart of the city stopped at another inn, where I had been once before and which was frequented by merchants and tradesmen. Here I made the acquaintance of a gentleman who spoke some English and from whom I learned that there were a number of printers in Cologne, the most prominent being Hiero Fuchs and Peter Quentel.

He gave me the addresses of both men, and I first went to the establishment of Hiero Fuchs, where I learned that he knew Tyndale but was not engaged in any work for him. I asked Fuchs if he thought that Tyndale might have a printing order at Peter Quentel's.

Fuchs was a big man with a sandy mustache that drooped down at the corners on either side of his mouth. At my question he licked out his tongue, pulled in a few hairs of this mustache, and began to chew upon them, looking at me suspiciously all the while. I am certain that he took me for an agent of the King's, at least some sort of spy or troublemaker.

"My name is Tom Barton," I explained, "and I am an English seaman trading out of London, Rotterdam, and Antwerp. Master Tyndale was a passenger on our ship last year. When he left us in Hamburg, he said that he'd be here in Cologne during this month having work done at a printer's."

What I was saying must have sounded like the truth because Fuchs ceased to chew upon his mustache; a kinder look came into his eyes. Still, he offered me grudging information.

"Tyndale I don't know," he said. "But the printing works of Peter Quentel are close by."

With this he took me by the arm, guided me into the street where my horse was tethered, and there with many gestures guided me on my way.

In spite of his instructions, after several misturnings and questionings of passersby, I at last found the Quentel print shop.

It stood on a dingy street close to the river, a narrow, run-down building with a fretwork gable and a dark entryway. In a cubbyhole beside the door that led to the printery sat an old woman knitting some sort of coarse garment from a spool of black wool. She was thin, the color of a potato sprout, and at her feet lay a small dog. The dog raised its head, growled at me, then stretched out again but continued to growl softly.

"What do you want of us?" the old lady asked, not lifting her eyes from her knitting.

"I wish to speak to Quentel," I said.

"This speaking you wish to do; what is it about?"

"About William Tyndale."

Now the woman raised her eyes and gave me a sharp glance, said something I did not understand, and went back to her knitting. I stood there on one foot and then the other. The knitting needles clicked back and forth; the dog had gone to sleep and was snoring.

"Who is this William Tyndale?" the woman asked after a while.

"An Englishman; a scholar," I said, unable to think of any other words to describe Tyndale. "He's printing a book . . ."

The woman reached up and pulled a cord, and far off somewhere I heard the jangle of a rusty bell.

Thereupon a door opened behind me, and I turned to see a tall man, whose clothes were splotched with printer's ink, standing there examining me. Behind him through the open door, I had a glimpse of the printing works with presses going, men crouched over them, and stacks of paper scattered around the floor. One of the men left a press where he was working and came over to the door. His hair, which stood straight up from his head, was spattered with ink.

It was William Tyndale. He recognized me at once though I had become somewhat broader in the year's time since we had seen each other and had grown a set of whiskers that made me look older than I would have otherwise.

Tyndale noticed them immediately.

"You've grown," he said. "You look like a regular sea captain now."

He was thin and stooped and pale, as if he had been living in a cellar.

"How do you fare with your reading?" he asked.

"Well," I said, exaggerating somewhat, "I'm moving along with the New Testament."

"Soon you'll be reading Italian and Spanish," Tyndale said.

He grasped my arm and introduced me to Peter Quentel, the gentleman who had barred my way and still stood in the door.

"There it is," said Tyndale, turning to point at the bundles of paper stacked beside the busy presses. He spoke with the excitement of a man who had just launched a three-masted ship.

"Come along and see what's been done."

Chapter 13

Tyndale went back to work at once. I think he had forgotten that I was there.

It was a difficult task he had set for himself. His text was written in English, and the workmen were Germans who neither spoke nor read English. There were also corrections to make in the manuscript and parleys with Quentel, a very particular printer. He had just purchased a new Gutenberg press, which still needed adjusting.

The translation was laid out on a workbench, the part that had already been printed in a neat stack, the rest in another. Hanging from ropes overhead were sheets pinned up to dry. The task seemed to be about half-finished, and Tyndale said that in another week they would begin working in quarto— whole sheets folded into four leaves. But the book would still be only half-finished, none of them complete and ready to ship.

There was nothing for me to do except to keep out of the way, send word to my uncle that the Bible was moving along, and wait until evening came and the printers quit. Tyndale wanted them to keep on by candlelight, but Quentel was firm against it.

"Not only the peasants are making trouble. It's all the workmen, too. If I were to ask them to work tonight, then tomorrow they'd not come until noon, perhaps not at all. They might even leave and go over to my competitor, Fuchs."

"You still have an idle press," Tyndale said. "Why can't it be used?"

"I have an order coming tomorrow," Quentel replied. "An important order from the former Dean at Mainz, Johann Dobneck, which I can't delay."

I noted a tall, limber-jointed young man, who had been running around the printery talking incessantly. His name was William Roye. He was an English friar, I learned, who had met Tyndale a few months before and had become his assistant.

Quentel soon herded all of us out, padlocked the big door, and bade us *gudenacht*. The old lady in the cubbyhole we left behind with her knitting and her blind dog. Apparently she lived there in her dark hole and acted as a servant by day and a watchman by night.

The talkative Friar Roye went on his way, arm and arm with two of the workmen, and Tyndale asked me to eat supper with him. Although I was hungry from my long day and was certain that his fare would be meager, I happily accepted his invitation. Leading my cart horse, I followed him along the embankment and on the way sent word to Uncle Jack in Antwerp by fast-sailing wherry to come at once. I knew he could not yet have finished taking on his cargo.

Tyndale's lodgings were not far distant from the printery, behind the cathedral, on a street so narrow that I had trouble getting my horse between the buildings. We went up a rickety staircase, up for five floors.

His quarters were bare except for a cot, a bench with pitcher, wash bowl, and brazier. A small, triangular window looked out at the square roof of the cathedral and a weathered working crane sitting atop it.

I spoke about the church as soon as he closed the door. Walking over to the window, he pried it open so that I could see better.

"That's why I took these lodgings," he said. "Because of the view. It's a great inspiration to me just to look out. I stand here and think of the men and women and children by the thousands who built the cathedral, working all of their lives, bringing stone from the quarries, cutting the stone, setting carved stone upon carved stone until the stones reached the sky. Do you know how many years it has taken to build the cathedral, and still it's not finished?"

"Fifty years," I said, making a guess.

"One hundred and ten years. Three generations of people have worked at it. When I get angry with myself for taking so much time, I think of their patience. I think of it but it doesn't do me considerable good. I'm still impatient. Now, at this moment, I'm impatient. We should be working tonight, every night, every hour, until the pages are printed and the book is bound and on its way to England."

"Have you been threatened?" I asked, wondering if some of his desire to get the task done might come from a feeling that he was in danger.

"Cologne isn't as free in its views as some other cities, but so far I've not been threatened."

"How about the old woman?"

"Who?"

"The old woman dressed in black who sits in the cubbyhole by the door and knits."

"I've never noticed her," Tyndale said.

He lighted the charcoal brazier under a pot of carrots and small pieces of gristly meat. The pot looked as if he had been eating from it for several days and the food, alas, confirmed my suspicions.

"Your assistant, Friar Roye," I said. "What of him? Is he trustworthy?"

"Oh, yes. I'd trust him with my life."

"He does a great amount of talking."

"That's his only fault. He is full of words, and they spill over frequently."

"I heard him brag to one of the workmen that your Bible would cause a revolution once it reached England. That in ten years the whole of England would become followers of the Lutheran faith."

"I've heard him say the same thing, and I've admonished him about it more than once. But he's full of enthusiasm. There's nothing I can do to stop his mouth."

It was cold. The fire in the brazier felt good. With the pot between us, we sat on the bench and helped ourselves, spooning out what we found afloat.

"How can you smuggle the Bibles into England?" Tyndale asked me.

"I've got a good plan, I think. Before, with the Luther pamphlets, I buried them in a bale of silk goods."

"I plan to print five thousand Bibles. They'll require a great number of bales. Too many, perhaps."

"That's my conclusion also. Therefore, the new plan. I'll gather up some large wine barrels—we'll have to make measurements—then we'll sit down and calculate. I'll also order the same number of small barrels. Into the small barrels we'll stack the Bibles and seal them moisture-tight. Then we'll fill the space between the two barrels with wine and seal them."

Tyndale smiled, apparently pleased with the plan. I smiled, too, pleased with myself for having thought of it.

"How is the reading? Does it progress?" Tyndale asked.

"I can read most anything," I bragged, not knowing that he was about to test me. "I studied the notes and the manuscript you left, and every day I've practiced. I've walked the deck of the ship and even the streets and read aloud to myself."

Tyndale got up and rummaged around in his string bag. He pulled out a sheet of paper and thrust it toward me.

"If you will, read this for me. I like to hear it. It's not that I doubt your word. I just like to listen. It's from Matthew, the first book I translated. The page is defective. Ink was spilled on it. But do your best and I'll listen carefully."

The light was poor. I was not familiar with the letters that Quentel used on his press, but I started to read and did my best:

> *Ye have heard how it is said: thou shalt love thine neighbor, and hate thine enemy. But I say unto you, love your enemies. Bless them that curse you. Do good to them that hate you. Pray for them which do you wrong and persecute you, that ye may be the children of your Father that is in heaven: for he maketh his sun to arise on the evil, and on the good, and sendeth his rain on the just and the unjust. For if ye love them, which love you: what reward shall ye have? Do not the publicans even so? And if ye be friendly to your brethren only: what singular thing do ye? Do not the publicans likewise? Ye shall therefore be perfect, even as your Father, which is in heaven, is perfect.*

"Good!" Tyndale exclaimed and clapped his hands. Then he gave me another paper to read, and still another, until my voice at last gave out.

"You'll be reading not only Spanish and Italian," he said, "but French as well."

He acted as if I were the best student he'd ever had. If the truth were known, I must have been the worst. But yet I was greatly pleased.

When the time came for me to leave, he asked me to stay. There was only one cot and, being certain that he would insist that I sleep on it while he slept on the floor, I said I must go. Besides, I was still very hungry. Sleep on my empty young stomach would be impossible.

"You've read enough for today," he said. "Many read too much, until the words run together and mean nothing. But don't forget to read tomorrow and, when you get through, think about what you've read. Not only think about it but take it into yourself as you take in the air you breathe."

I mounted my horse and threaded my way down the unlighted street. At the first turning, where three lanes came together and formed a wide place, two men were standing.

One was holding a small lantern. He was young and handsome, with a feathered hat and his hair in curls. He glanced at my awkward cart horse and made a slighting remark about it that I failed to hear completely.

The other man laughed. He was half-turned from me, but in the dull glow of the lantern I saw part of him. I saw enough. The laughter I had heard before.

They gave me a nasty surprise that lasted while I sat down and tried hard to eat some lamb shanks and cabbage. Then, as I lay half-awake, it lasted until morning came.

Could the man I had seen by lantern light really be Herbert Belsey? Could Belsey have survived the fight with my uncle? And if he had survived, could he possibly have reached the mainland shore? To say the truth, the thought that Belsey was still alive gave me a shock. It was like an iron vise gripping my chest.

Chapter 14

In the morning I went straight to Quentel's on foot, deeming this a quicker way of travel than by cart horse.

I found the printery filled with workmen, the Dobneck order having come in. Tyndale was busy at one of the three presses, but I drew him aside and asked him if he had seen Herbert Belsey since coming to Cologne.

"Yes," Tyndale said. "This very morning."

"Are you certain it was Belsey?"

"Yes. He was leaving the cathedral."

"Did he speak?"

"No, but it was Herbert Belsey."

"It couldn't be someone who looks like him?"

"Not many people do. No, I am certain that the man I saw was Belsey."

"Did he follow you?"

"Probably, though I didn't watch to see."

"What are we to do about him?"

"Nothing. Except to hurry the Bible through the press," Tyndale said.

I went off at once in search of the old woman, who knew the city's secrets, and was told that I would find her at the cathedral, where she had an early morning chore of changing the altar candles.

I found her there, moving around in her black cloak, a pair of sharp cutting shears dangling from her waist, a basket in either hand, one holding fresh candles and the other burned-out stubs.

"Have you seen a tall man with lank hair hanging down his neck?" I asked her. "A man with a long, pale-colored nose turned up at the end?"

"Pale?" the old woman said. "I've never seen such a nose. Pale? Turned up at the end? Never."

"His name is Belsey. Herbert Belsey."

"I haven't seen such a man."

"You may. Today or tomorrow," I said. "If you do, if he comes to the printery, let me know at once. It will be worth your while."

Dropping a coin into each of her baskets, I took my leave of the old woman and began a stroll through the church, on the chance that I might encounter Belsey.

What I would do should I meet this fanatical searcher, I didn't know. Should I caution him not to molest Tyndale? Should I challenge him on the spot as Uncle Jack would have done? Should I fix him with a warning glance, and ignore him further?

It was early, the sun scarce shining through the windows of the eastern transept.

I passed worshippers kneeling at the small chapels, workmen chipping away at the stone floor with hammer and chisel, and a man setting new tile. I walked quickly through the church, casting my eye here and there. Belsey was not about. I looked for him outside and as I made my way down the street toward the river and Quentel's shop, to no avail.

The Rhine was silver in the morning light. Carts were unloading baskets filled with fruit and vegetables, and women were setting them out on trestles in an open market near the printery. I paused there to buy three French pears for my breakfast, walked on to the river bank, and ate them.

Keeping an eye out meanwhile for Belsey, I returned by way of the market, which was now crowded with early shoppers. Belsey was not among them, but he could not be far off. The city was huddled around the cathedral and market in a tight semicircle. We would meet soon enough.

I hoped that Uncle Jack would arrive in Cologne before we did.

Chapter 15

The attack upon Tyndale that we both expected came not from Belsey nor from any of the King's many agents. It came from Johann Dobneck.

The attack had already begun when, leaving the marketplace, I walked into Quentel's and found the press, which hitherto had been idle, now attended by four printers and a short, thin-visaged but important-looking individual in a scholar's gown. This was Dobneck.

Dobneck was the former Dean of the principal church in Frankfurt-am-Main.

During the peasant revolt against the barons and clergy, he had been driven out of his church and had fled across the river to the town of Mainz. Again set upon by the peasants, he had escaped with his life by fleeing down the Rhine to Cologne, where he now resided.

He was a venomous enemy of Martin Luther's, therefore, upon whose preachments he rightly blamed his recent misfortune. And though Dobneck had never met Tyndale, the fact that Tyndale was Luther's friend made him an enemy also.

Once the typesetters had begun work on Dobneck's manuscript, the Dean strolled over to the press where Tyndale and I were standing. Introducing himself, he glanced at the printed sheets above his head, hung up to dry. Apparently he could read no English for he then smiled, mumbled a brief courtesy, and returned to his own work, which judging by his walk was of the greatest concern.

Little did Dobneck know that there around him in the very room where he now was bustling about, lying upon the bed of the press, hanging aloft above his head, were the parts of a book that, the mere thought of which ere the day was out, would make his eyes roll in his head.

We thought that it must have been William Roye who some time during that day gave him the clue, although we never could be certain.

Suffice it to say that when the printers quit work at nightfall Dean Dobneck invited them all to his quarters a short distance up the street to celebrate the completion of the first day's work on his manuscript.

There Dobneck got them bousy. When the time came to part, he asked the bousiest of the artisans to stay behind. This was a man named Kurtz, who, with promptings and questions from Dobneck, confessed that in the printery house at that moment was an order for five thousand copies of the New Testament translated into English from the Greek language.

Kurtz also confessed that a group of English merchants located in Antwerp, who had advanced the money for the project, planned to smuggle the Bibles into England before the King or Cardinal could lay a hand upon them.

Furthermore, said Kurtz, William Roye had bragged to him time and again, while the printing was going on, that once the Tyndale Bible reached England and was read by the populace, the whole country would rise up in revolt.

Dobneck's party took place on a Tuesday night. Early two mornings later I heard about it from the old woman, whom I met by chance as she was coming out of the cathedral. She wore a black shawl over her head, and I didn't recognize her until she spoke. Even then I wasn't sure who she might be, so excited was her speech.

"Have you heard about Meister Kurtz?" she asked. "Meister Kurtz, the printer. You know him. He's the one with the long beard that keeps getting caught in everything."

"Did he catch it again?" I asked.

"No," she said, brushing the rusty shawl away from her face. "It's worse than that. He caught himself."

"Himself?" I was beginning to wonder if the old lady was daft.

"Yes," she said, putting her basket of candle ends on the pavement. "At the party he blabbed his mouth to Dean Dobneck. Told him all about the Bible and how Meister Tyndale and Meister Roye and you are going to smuggle it into England and cause a lot of trouble with the people."

"He just repeated what Roye has been bragging about for some time."

The old lady took a step in my direction and, though there was no one near us except a flock of pigeons, lowered her voice.

"But not to Dean Dobneck, he hasn't said anything. Meister Dobneck's eyes rolled around in his head when he heard it. Around and around, I can tell you."

"How do you know they rolled around and around? How do you know all this?"

"I saw it. I was close enough to reach out and touch Meister Dobneck when he told Meister Quentel what Meister Kurtz had told him."

"What did Meister Quentel say?" I asked, suspicious for the first time that something might be amiss.

"Nothing. He said nothing. He just stood there and looked at Meister Dobneck."

"Where did all this go on? I've been in the printery every day since Dobneck came."

"In Meister Quentel's office."

"Then what happened?"

"Meister Quentel said he had heard all that talk before. The Dean said, 'What are you going to do about it?'"

"'Nothing,' Meister Quentel said. 'This is a free city, and I can print what it pleases me to print.'"

The old woman, seeming to forget that I was there, reached into her cloak and took out some crusts of bread and tossed them around to the pigeons.

"What happened then?" I prompted her.

"A regular ruckus, is what. When Meister Quentel said that it was a free city and he'd print what pleased him, the Dean swore a terrible oath."

"Then what?"

"Then Meister Dobneck said, 'I'll go to the Diet of Cologne. To my friend, who is a leader there, and have the Diet issue an order to seize the Bible you're printing and everything pertaining to it—manuscript, paper, ink—everything. I'll go at once.'"

"What did Meister Quentel do?"

"He said, 'Go to the Diet. I have friends there also.' Then the Dean said, 'I'll take my order out of your shop.' 'Do so,' said Meister Quentel. 'The sooner the better.'"

"Is that all? Did it end there?"

"It's not ended," the old woman said. "Meister Dobneck did leave at once to see his friend in the Diet, and the Diet is to meet this afternoon. I heard it just this morning, a moment ago when the sacristan asked me to put flowers in the chapel where they hold their meetings. I'm on my way now to buy flowers at the market to put in the chapel. The sacristan gave me fifty pfennigs, and I can keep ten. That's the arrangement we have. It's always that way between us."

The old lady went waddling off down the slope toward the marketplace. A cold wind blowing up from the river reminded me to settle deeper into my cloak.

I went into the cathedral to wait until the old lady returned with the flowers. I had decided to locate the chapel where the Diet, the governing body of Cologne, would meet that afternoon.

I had no plan as I sat there in the cathedral, only the inkling of one—the conviction that, if the old woman had spoken the truth, both Tyndale and I were in trouble.

Fortunately, although I was not to learn of it for two days, Uncle Jack arrived in Cologne at daylight of the next day.

Chapter 16

After a time the old woman came with a basket of flowers and arranged them in a chapel near the West Choir, the quietest part of the cathedral.

The meeting of the Diet, she informed me, had been delayed because three of its members were away in Frankfurt. Instead, the meeting would be held late in the afternoon of the following day.

It was early, but Tyndale was already at the printery, busy at work though none of the printers had yet arrived. He was bent over a table, goose quill in hand, making corrections on a page of manuscript. I had a difficult time gaining his attention.

"We're in trouble," I said, and repeated the words a third time before he heard me.

Only then did he pause and glance up. His eyes, however, had a far-off look in them, so I waited for a moment or two before I told him, as best I could remember, what the old woman had told me. I also told him about the argument between Dean Dobneck and Peter Quentel.

"I've just come from the cathedral," I said. "The old woman is arranging flowers for the meeting tomorrow afternoon. Dobneck has powerful friends in the Diet. He himself is powerful. We should make preparations now against the chance that the Diet decides to seize the printing."

As the first of the artisans came in, Tyndale laid down his pen and drew me into a corner of the shop where we could talk without being overheard.

"I doubt that the Diet will attack us," he said, "but I agree with you that we should be prepared. The printing is almost finished. It would be a catastrophe to lose it now."

"You can lose more than your Bible. If the Diet wishes, it can arrest you as a heretic. You could even lose your life."

Shrugging off the danger to himself, he said, "I can move quickly. I've moved quickly before. I can go upriver to Worms, where I thought of going before I came here. What do you suggest? How should I go? By cart and horse? By barge? By river boat?"

"Boat may be faster," I said. "On the other hand, the river is low and we could go aground."

"You say 'we.' Does that mean you are . . . ?"

"That's what I mean," I broke in.

I had never really declared myself to him before, but I admired and loved this frail little man, standing there before me, perplexed and fearful of what might happen to his books. I would do, I decided, anything to save him and his work.

"We're in this together. I'll go now and learn what I can."

I left forthwith and went down to the customs house, where I talked to several boatmen who had come from Worms and Mainz within the last few days.

They all agreed that the fastest way to Worms was by barge as far as the city of Mainz, but from there on they advised horse and cart.

A quick departure from Cologne was equally important. Should the Diet issue an order for seizure on the following afternoon, we should be ready to leave the city not more than a few hours later, by midnight at the latest.

The search for transportation took up most of the day. In the end I found a river boat and a barge, suitable for us and our cargo, and paid a small deposit to their owners to ensure space.

I then went to a cooper and purchased twenty wine barrels, ten small ones and ten large, which we would need in either case—should we be forced to flee the city or should the printing continue unmolested and the barrels be needed for storage.

I reached the printery just before it closed for the day. True to his promise, Dean Dobneck had packed up his manuscript that morning and left. On his way out, he again threatened Quentel with severe penalties if he continued with the Bible. Quentel appeared to be undisturbed.

"Dobneck will get nowhere," he said. "A cohort of his, Hermann Rinck, came here today to snoop around and ask questions. Rinck is a senator of Cologne and a knight, powerful therefore in the Diet, but I doubt that he will act against us."

Quentel spoke with more confidence than I myself felt. That a senator of the Diet had come to the printery to look around at the behest of Dobneck was even more disturbing to me than the fact that Dobneck had canceled his printing order.

I walked homeward with Tyndale. I told him about the cargo space I had arranged for and my purchase of the twenty barrels. Tyndale shared Quentel's confidence that the Diet would not interfere, especially that he was in no danger himself.

"I am not at all sure," I said. "I think everything is in danger—you—your work—Quentel—myself—everything."

Tyndale gave me a questioning look. "Are you certain you want to go through with this? There is danger, I'll admit. You're a young man, not a scholar; a seaman . . ."

"You talk as if you were my grandfather when you're not very much older than I. We're in this together, as I've said before. Together."

As we parted, he said, "Now that Dobneck has taken himself off, Quentel has promised me the use of another press. With two presses at work I should be finished within a month or less."

"I'll go ahead with my plans anyway. Just as though we had to leave the city at an hour's notice. In the middle of the night, if need be."

"Pray God we won't need to."

To my eyes, Tyndale looked sick, but he bounded away from me and started up the five flights to his garret as if he were a brawny sailor climbing a mast.

Night was approaching as I walked away, my thoughts on the morrow, when I saw a tall figure, a man whose walk I recognized. He was at a distance, close upon the river, moving past a brace of barges moored near in. I was certain that it was Herbert Belsey, whom, in the confusion of the day, I had forgotten.

Changing my direction, I moved quickly down the embankment, but by the time I reached the river Belsey had disappeared. I lingered there on the landing stairs for a while, thinking that he might return.

That he was still following Tyndale was certain. This, besides the threat from Johann Dobneck, was not a comforting thought.

Could Belsey have dropped the clue about Tyndale's Bible? I wondered. Was it Belsey who had first alarmed Dobneck and sent him running off to alert the Diet?

Chapter 17

Standing there on the landing stairs while I turned these thoughts over in my mind, I was surprised when Belsey appeared quietly at my side.

"I hope you're not taken aback," he said. "If you are, it's understandable. But I'm not a shade come to haunt you."

With that he stepped closer and touched my sleeve, as if to prove he was really flesh and blood, not an apparition.

"I've seen you before," I said, drawing away. "Here in Cologne when I first came to the city."

The door of a nearby inn opened and closed. In the brief interval a dim light shone out from the inn and fell upon him.

I had a fleeting glimpse of a face that was greatly changed from the last time I had seen it—at that moment when my uncle had grasped Belsey and flung him against the rail, then, as he lay stunned, staring up at the sky, had lifted him and shoved his body across the rail and out into the sea. His mouth was twisted to one side by a scar that ran from chin to temple.

"What do you want of us?" I asked him.

"Only what is due me," he answered. "And to good King Henry the Eighth."

There was a slur in his speech that I had never heard before.

"What is due, whatever you think is due, you are risking your life to get it," I said. "My uncle will put an end to you one of these days."

"And King Henry will put an end to him. The King has a long arm, and many of them."

"Like an octopus?"

"Exactly."

The current was sucking away at the inner bank, making a noise that drowned out his next words, but I didn't ask him to repeat them.

"If I tell my uncle that you're in Cologne," I said, "that you are alive, following him around, he'll hunt you out and slit your throat."

"Now you wouldn't do a thoughtless thing like that, would you, young sir?" Belsey said, taking on a hurt tone. "Not after all I've been through, floating through the fog, clinging to an abandoned cask for hours, floating half-dead to shore, lying among the rocks washed by the waves . . ."

Belsey fell silent, hunched against the river cold.

"Where's your ship?" he asked suddenly.

"In the Lowlands," I said. "I don't know where Uncle Jack moored her."

"She could be in Rotterdam or Antwerp or Amsterdam or a hundred other places between for all you know."

"She could," I said.

"It surprises me that you don't know where your own ship lies. If I owned a nice three-master like the *Black Pearl,* I'd know where she was, I can tell you."

"She's not my ship," I said. "And if she were and I knew where she lay, I still would keep it to myself."

Belsey drew deeper into his cloak as the inn door opened again. The light shone on him briefly, revealing his twisted face. For an instant, and strongly against my will, I felt a twinge of sympathy for the man. I thought of the Bible words I had read to Tyndale.

When the inn door closed and it was dark again, Belsey said, "I was thinking that, since you own the *Black Pearl,* that you and I, the two of us, could get together in a trading venture . . . "

"Why do you keep repeating that the ship is mine when you well know that she is not mine? She belongs to my uncle, Jack Barton."

"Since you ask, I'll tell you. Because, young mate, she does belong to you. The certificate of ownership is a forgery. Forged by your Uncle Jack. I can prove it so from the *Book of Ships* in the Port of London.

"Your father, Thomas Barton, had one brother whose name was Jack—the man you call Uncle Jack."

" 'Tis true."

"Your father died of the plague in the year fifteen-twenty, and also your mother. You were then aged twelve."

"It's a sad memory."

"And your father at the time of his death owned a ship called the *Trident*."

"Yes, I remember. I sailed on the ship once as far on the river as London. My father took me on my birthday."

"The *Trident,* by terms of your father's will, was placed in the name of his brother, Jack, to keep in trust for you until you reached the age of sixteen."

"I know nothing of the will you mention."

"That's quite obvious, young sir. Nor would I expect you to, being as you were at the time of a tender age. And manipulations happening since of which you're unaware."

A barge went by, and he waited for a moment. "Dr. Kinkade," Belsey said, "was at your father's bedside when he died and read the original will. That's why I know that one existed."

Another barge passed slowly by close in upon the shore, and the bargeman called out a greeting. His words hung for a while in the heavy air, but neither of us answered.

Belsey said, "You're seventeen and have been for some ten months. But the ship has not yet been transferred to your ownership as your father's will directed it should be. I know this because I ran across the facts while searching a different matter. Quite by chance, I may add."

"It's hard to believe the things you say," I broke in. "They don't sound like things my Uncle Jack would do."

Belsey gave a muffled snort. "Your uncle may be God-fearing, and he should be, if you ask me. He should fear God, God's great wrath, for many reasons. For one, his being a heretical sniveler after Martin Luther. Another, for being the wiliest smuggler on the River Thames."

"You speak poorly of my uncle in his absence," I said, my anger rising. "Would you speak so in his presence?"

"Knowing him also as a potential murderer," Belsey replied, "I doubt that I would. But that doesn't alter the facts, only the circumstances. It bespeaks a cowardly caution on my part, nothing else."

"You have a grudge against my uncle, that's clear. You'd say anything against him that came to mind."

"A grudge? Who could blame me if I did? But it's not a grudge I bear. Long before Jack Barton heaved me overboard, thinking all the time that it was to my death, long ere this I learned the facts of your father's will. I had my eye on your uncle when he came in from Antwerp last January and cheated the King out of his rightful revenues by loading his cargo at two o'clock on a Sunday morning at Saint Catherine's Way and carting it off before daylight. I had my eye on him, and I went to Sheerness and looked into the local records. That's how I know the facts, why the *Black Pearl* is yours, though Jack Barton acts otherwise."

"I'm sure that my uncle plans to transfer the ship into my name as soon as we return to London." I said this although I had had no such assurance.

"That's good to hear," Belsey answered. "Now we can talk to the point. I have lodging at the Blue Heron Inn. Come by tomorrow afternoon, and we'll explore things further."

With that he started up the landing stairs. Halfway to the top, he paused and turned around.

"Between times," he said, "you might give thought to some important matters. I know, for instance, that Tyndale is in Cologne. I know that the Bible he's printing is half-finished, at the least. I am also aware that you and your uncle plan to help him in a diabolical scheme, using the *Black Pearl,* to smuggle the heretical book into England."

A barge went past, towed by a team of four horses, and Belsey waited until it was quiet again.

"Do you wish to have the *Black Pearl* seized?" he said. "For seize it we shall. It's one thing for Jack Barton to lose a ship. But it's quite another to lose a ship that otherwise would be your own. It's something that you may wish to think about before we meet tomorrow. Don't you agree?"

I said nothing, too confused to think of a reply. Belsey went quietly up the stairs and off toward the city, moving silently over the cobbles with his light, peculiar stride.

I watched him go, so shaken by the news he had just imparted that when I began to climb the stairs I had to stop halfway up to find my breath, to gather my strength, and even to remember where I lived.

Chapter 18

Close upon dawn I went to the market and rummaged through piles of old clothes.

I purchased a pair of down-at-the-heel boots, a patched, woolen smock, and a big-brimmed, well-worn hat of braided straw. It was an artisan's outfit—one that could be seen on anyone who worked with his hands—a bargeman, a water carrier, or a carpenter. I also purchased a wooden bucket, a trowel, and a chipping hammer.

An hour before the Diet was to meet, I changed into the old clothes and with my tools went to the cathedral. I filled my bucket at one of the wells and made my way to the chapel that the old woman had decorated with flowers.

There were a hundred or more artisans of all skills at work in the great cathedral, painting, setting tile, busy at sundry other activities. One more artisan, I had concluded, would not be noticed.

I surveyed the chapel thoroughly, locating the position of the presiding officer by a chair and table placed halfway to the back.

The chapel was small, not more than thirty feet in length. If I took up a position near the entrance, beside one of the pillars, I would be able to see and hear all that went on inside.

The pillar sat upon a base constructed of six stone slabs. The joints between the slabs were ragged in places and upon them I set to work, having first watched an artisan repairing similar cracks in a chapel at the opposite side of the cathedral.

The Diet came together as the church bells tolled the hour of three.

The members filled the small chapel, and several of the men were forced to stand, not an arm's length from where I had already set about filling, after a fashion, the cracks in the stone pedestal. Most of them seemed to be men of business, well-fed and richly dressed, but at least six were churchmen.

After the reading of two long papers, Dobneck was acknowledged by the presiding official. The official called him

not Dean Dobneck but Meister Cochlaeus, a Latin literary name, which he seemed to like better than plain Dobneck.

Jumping to his feet, Dobneck cleared his throat, cleared it twice. He was a small man and had a pinched face.

William Roye called him a "pratly little poad."

He cleared his throat for a third time and then launched forth against Tyndale. At first his voice was soft, but it soon climbed to a pitch that I could easily hear over the tap, tap of my hammer as I chiseled away at the crumbled seams of the pedestal. My German speech was halting, but I understood the language when I heard it. I understood everything Dobneck was saying.

"When I found," he said, "that this English heretic was printing a devil-inspired tract here under our very noses, I asked my dear friend Senator Rinck to investigate. What he discovered he will inform you when I have finished."

Two men in uniform were standing on either side of the chapel door, holding tall staffs made of gold and ivory. Once when Dean Dobneck paused in his tirade and quiet fell in the chapel, one of the men gave me a poke on the bottom, ordering me to use my hammer with less enthusiasm.

Half-listening to Dobneck, I chipped away with hammer and chisel, sluiced out the cracks with my bucket of water, made myself look workmanlike and busy while I counted the seconds until he finished.

Senator Rinck then arose and said that he had sent a friend to the Quentel printery where the friend found great quantities of paper lying about and every evidence that something was afoot.

At five o'clock by the church bells the Diet voted. The vote was unanimous. And by it a prohibition was placed upon Quentel against proceeding further with the Tyndale Bible.

Shortly after the vote was announced, I picked up my bucket and walked quietly down the long nave of the cathedral and outside. There at the door I emptied the bucket of water and taking the old Roman road came quickly to the printery.

Quentel was away somewhere on business, but I called Tyndale aside and told him that the Diet had voted against us.

"You're certain?"

"The clerk has already started to draw up the prohibition," I said. "Rinck was standing over him, telling him what to say, and the clerk was putting it down. We're safe until daylight. But not an hour more."

"It'll take hours to pack my papers," Tyndale said.

"The ship leaves around midnight, the barge at daybreak. You'll need to pack in a hurry."

"But I can't begin until the printers quit work."

"It's better if we can catch the ship. The barge leaves six hours later and it's slower. I'll go out now and hire horse and cart and be back here shortly after dark. I can help you then, and perhaps we can get Quentel and the old woman to help, too."

I quickly surveyed the shop. Paper was scattered everywhere. The cords strung overhead were filled with wet pages hung up to dry. Men were working at all three of the presses.

"It may be wise," I said, "to leave everything just as it is. Leave everything behind, except your manuscript. Dobneck wants to stop the printing but, even more, he wants to get his hands on you."

"I'll have to take the chance," Tyndale said.

It was the gentleness of this man that attracted me to him. It had not come at once, not on the voyage to Hamburg, not of a sudden, not like a blinding light, but slowly over the weeks we had been together. And now, as he stood there smudged with printer's grime, calmly facing the destruction of his year's work, I felt bound to him more than ever.

"I'll go now to look for a cart and collect the barrels," I said. "It may take me an hour or more."

First, having heard that Uncle Jack had arrived in Cologne, I went looking for him. I found him at a riverfront inn, holding forth with a small group of river men. I motioned him aside and told him what had happened at the meeting of the Diet and about my talk with Tyndale.

"I'm on my way now to find a horse and cart. We have a barge waiting, but we'll need to hurry."

Uncle Jack struck a fist into the palm of a hand. He was always striking something. Himself; someone else. With an amiable crack on the shoulder. When no one was near, he would strike an object a terrible blow—a chair, a table, a lamp.

"We'll fool them, Tom. Fool them, eh?"

"I've seen Belsey," I blurted out.

"Belsey?"

Uncle Jack spoke the name as if he had never heard it before.

"Herbert Belsey?" he croaked, as if there were more Belseys than one in the world. "Alive? Here in Cologne?"

He struck a nearby barrel so hard that the top cracked and the barrel began to roll toward the river.

Chapter 19

Packing took longer than we had planned. As midnight approached, I ran down to the embankment and asked the shipowner to delay his sailing.

This he refused to do, answering me in such an unfriendly way as to arouse my suspicions that he might have heard of the Diet's intent to seize Tyndale. The bargeman, on the other hand, glad to pick up added freightage, promised to wait until we came—whatever time it might be.

An hour before dawn we had the twenty barrels loaded on the cart, half of them filled with printed sheets, and were on our way.

The cart had iron-shod wheels, and the horse was also shod with iron. We made a dreadful racket in the quiet streets, therefore, added to by the barking of dogs, a sound so dreadful, indeed, that I half-expected to be pounced upon by the law long ere we reached the river.

To our good fortune the Rhine was at a height that made it possible to drive the cart directly onto the barge. There, securely tied down alongside two other carts, we awaited the dawn, still expecting to be seized.

Dawn broke clear with a promise of fine weather and, since it was the month of September, the river was at its lowest and ran for the most part at a pawky rate. Using six stout horses in tandems of two and four men to pole, the bargeman made good time and without mishap brought us safely on the morning of the seventh day to the landing place, where the river divides and forms a marshy island near the main gate into Worms.

Here we drove our cart ashore, and Uncle Jack left me to watch over it and went into the town with Tyndale to search for someone who would be willing to undertake the job we had failed to finish at Cologne. In midafternoon they returned in a jubilant mood.

"A printer! A printer!" Uncle Jack shouted when still a hundred strides away. "We've found a printer!"

The printer was Peter Schoeffer, and his shop was located at a short distance from the main gate.

Driving the cart thither, Uncle Jack at the reins, Tyndale and I afoot, we passed through a large crowd in the town square, it being market day.

People stopped to stare at us, thinking perhaps from our English countenances and strange garb that we might be a troupe of traveling mummers. There were many catcalls and questions, some of which Uncle Jack answered good-naturedly in his stentorian voice. One grizzled lout wanted to know what we were hiding in the barrels. In answer my uncle shouted, "Worms." But on the whole the townspeople were friendly.

"What thinkest of Belsey?" Uncle Jack asked me.

"I think he's in Cologne," I said, remembering for the first time in days that Belsey had asked me to come see him and talk about the ship.

Chapter 20

No sooner had we unloaded our cart at Schoeffer's print shop than Uncle Jack took me by the arm and led me into the street, leaving Tyndale behind to start the work.

"Tyndale," Uncle Jack said, "learned this afternoon that the sheets we carted up the river can't be used because Schoeffer doesn't have the type to match them. So he's starting over from the beginning. The beginning, mind you. This time he'll print a different sized Bible, a smaller Bible, which he calls an octavo. The sheets that he printed in Cologne I'll take with me tomorrow. Tomorrow morning."

"Tomorrow?"

"Yes, I have passage on a ship leaving for the coast. When I reach Antwerp, once I have the *Black Pearl* in condition, I'll make a run for England. A month from now the sheets will be selling at Paul's Cross."

"What am I to do while you're gone?"

"Help Tyndale with the new printing, of course. He'll need your help. The sheets I take with me now will serve to whet the public's appetite. The finished Bible, which you will bring along at year's end, will cause a furor. A furor. Perhaps, as William Roye says, 'a revolution.' Yes, a revolution. How does that strike you? Eh?"

It came to me then, at that moment, to speak up about the ship, to blurt out everything I had learned from Herbert Belsey. In truth, this urge to confront my uncle, to state the rights I held to my father's ship, had been upon me every day of our journey from Cologne.

I remained silent then, however, and I remained silent now as we stood facing each other in the cold wind. My silence must have come from long years of obedience to Uncle Jack. Yes, and physical fear, too; of what he might do to me should I arouse him.

It came also from my doubts concerning Belsey. Had he told me the truth about the inheritance? Was his story the first step in an effort to get his hands on the *Black Pearl?* Was it part of a scheme to seize Tyndale's Bible, even Tyndale himself? Was it the means by which Uncle Jack and I would land in prison? Could it be a combination of all of these things that inspired Herbert Belsey to seek out and confide in me?

"Of a sudden, you show me a hangdog face," Uncle Jack said. "You should be happy. Happy! What a privilege you have now. Rare, I say. To help in a great cause. A great cause, eh?"

Still I stood in sullen silence, my back turned to the biting wind, thinking that now was the time for me to speak.

"It is my wish to go to sea again," I said at last.

Uncle Jack gave me a nudge with his heavy fist. "Sure you do, Tom. You're a sailor through and through. But you'll be going to sea soon enough. When the Bible is printed, you'll be on your way to England. On your way."

"It took a long time in Cologne and all for nothing," I replied. "And it may take a long time here and come to nothing again."

"I'll get the ship ready, Tom. She needs to be hauled and inspected stem to stern. She'll need paint. A new sail or two. Sounds good to you, Tom, I can see. Good, eh?"

"I wish to go with you and come back later, after we get the ship ready."

Not my words but something in my voice must have alerted Uncle Jack. Around the corner of his mouth a small muscle suddenly began to twitch.

"Well," he said, taking his time about it, "we can't both go and leave Master Tyndale here alone by himself. Leave him alone. Couldn't do that, could we, Tom, eh?"

"I don't see the good of loafing around here for three months or more when I can go and come back. I'm not a printer, you know. And as for friends, he's got William Roye."

"He and Roye don't see eye to eye, not since Roye went around Cologne bragging his head off. But the friendship's not important. Not important. You forget that this is a business venture we have with Tyndale. If we both go traipsing off, what's to prevent someone from coming in and cutting us out? The ship's been tied up for more than a month now. By the time I reach Antwerp, it will be close on to two months. We have a lot of money invested in this venture. That's the straight of it. You can see, Tom, why I have to get along and you must stay to see that everything goes right. That we don't get cheated out of our rightful due. Our due."

Uncle Jack, his great shoulders hunched against the wind, his brow furrowed, and his black eyes darting, waited impatiently for me to speak.

It was on my tongue to say, "I'll go to Antwerp and you, Uncle Jack, can stay here. Do you understand?"

But my old fear of him, my doubts concerning Belsey, froze the words in my throat. Shuffling my feet on the cold stones in an astonishment of fear and indecision, I painfully remained silent.

Uncle Jack said, "A fine arrangement as you will see, Tom. Fine. Fine arrangement, eh?"

I did not answer.

That evening until the bells struck midnight we worked packing the printed sheets of Tyndale's unfinished Bible into the barrels.

At dawn Uncle Jack started down the Rhine with them on his long voyage to London.

Tyndale came up as I stood there in the cold dawn. He must have known how I felt, my loneliness for my ship and the sea. But he said nothing, letting my emotions be what they were.

After a while he said, "Let's walk up to the cathedral. It's a wondrous place."

The cathedral sat on a rise, the highest ground in the country thereabouts. The houses of the town clustered around it, like a brood of brown and white chicks. Cathedral and town were enclosed by two walls, the first built by the Romans when they conquered this part of the world and the second wall in later days. The cathedral itself, though smaller than the cathedral in Cologne, yet filled the eyes with its two large domes and four round towers of darksome stone.

Close by the cathedral was the Pfalz, a building that served as the bishop's quarters. It was here that the Emperor lived during his stay in Worms and here also, in one of the rooms upstairs, where Martin Luther went to trial.

Tyndale took me to this place and opened the door upon a long room decorated with banners and emblems.

"Tom," he said, "where you stand, in October, four years ago, stood Martin Luther. And here in front of you, not ten strides away, sat the great Emperor of the Holy Roman Empire and six electors—an awesome court of princes and nobles, prelates and townspeople. The Diet of Worms had come to sit in judgment upon Luther. He was asked by the Emperor to recant all of the heresies he had written and preached in his lifetime. Luther hesitated, looked this way and that, then faced Charles the Fifth, the most powerful man on earth, more powerful than the King of England, and replied, 'I cannot and will not recant anything. Here I stand. I can do no other. God help me. Amen.'"

His voice trailed off. He put his arm around my shoulders, and together we left the cathedral. Night was falling, and it was bitter cold, but he stopped and once more looked down upon me, benevolently and hopefully, as a loving friend might do.

BOOK THREE

Chapter 21

We heard no news from Uncle Jack until more than three months had passed.

An Antwerp merchant, who traded along the river in English woolens, came to Schoeffer's print shop one cold morning early in December and asked for Tom Barton.

When I identified myself, he handed over a letter sealed with two blobs of bright red wax, addressed to me in my uncle's crabbed handwriting. I asked the merchant how he had come by the letter, to which he gave me an evasive answer, bowed politely, and, as if he were being spied upon, quickly disappeared.

Written on the twentieth day of November from the English Adventurers' warehouse in Antwerp, the letter read:

My Dear Nephew Tom—

You will be cheered to learn that our transaction has met with success. Our thirty lengths of Cologne silk found a ready market and the merchants who bought them clamored fulsomely for more, which I have promised them ere the middle of the near year. God approving, I'll await you here in a month's time. Should you be longer in gathering a new shipment of silk, send me a message at the address you will note above. Praise the Lord!

Your loving,
Uncle Jack.

I read the letter to Tyndale, slowly, because Uncle Jack despite his great dimensions wrote a small chick-track hand. Both of us rejoiced to learn that the sheets printed in Cologne had reached England safely and found an enthusiastic market in London. I rejoiced also because at last I could read my uncle's writing, anyone's writing.

There was no need to answer the letter; the Bible was completed three days after its arrival. Since the printing was almost twice the size of the first one, some five thousand copies, we decided to pack half of the Bibles in barrels and half in bales of leather aprons from the local marketplace.

We were held up three days because of violent winds and rain, but on the third day set forth down the swollen Rhine.

Delayed neither at the customs castle nor at Cologne, which we contrived with the help of the boat captain to pass during the night, we made good time, arriving at Rotterdam, and sailing west to Antwerp before the month was out. Nowhere, though a sharp lookout was kept, did we see Herbert Belsey, the searcher.

Uncle Jack, as he had promised, was waiting for us at the English Adventurers' warehouse, where he helped us store four thousand copies of the new printing. Then at once we set about transferring the remainder of our cargo to the *Black Pearl*.

It took a week's time to repack for storage and to stow the other cumbersome crates and barrels against the rough weather we were certain to encounter on our voyage to England. We had decided on this course lest any harm befall the ship and all the Bibles be lost.

The day of our sailing dawned bleak, with low, scurrying clouds and a rising wind. By noon, when we were ready to sail except for battening down, the wind had gained force. We stood, the three of us, in the lee of the roundhouse, surveying the skies and the murky waters.

Tyndale said, "It might be wise to wait for a better day."

"This time of year," Uncle Jack said, "there are no better days. The days grow worse, if anything. Worse. Eh, Tom?"

"I doubt they'll be worse," I said.

Not expecting this answer, Uncle Jack blinked.

In all of my days with Uncle Jack, since the time I was a cabin boy at the age of twelve, I had never gainsaid him on ship matters, not once, little enough on other matters. But the knowledge that the *Black Pearl* belonged to me, that I was now the owner and, if I wished to be, her master, emboldened me to say, "I favor waiting. Not alone for the safety of our cargo but also for the safety of the ship."

I doubt that Uncle Jack believed he had heard me rightly. At least his mouth came open and stayed open until I said, "There's usually a break between storms of three or four days. We should wait."

"I've sailed the Channel ere you were born, Tom Barton. Don't tell me when to sail or when not to sail."

"I don't tell you when or when not," I answered, still emboldened. "It is my opinion that we should wait, and I offer it for its worth."

"Worth nothing," Uncle Jack said. "Nothing. And what's more, I did not ask for an opinion." To show his resolve, he shouted orders to the carpenter, who stood in the waist ready to batten down.

"We're in danger lying here," he said, addressing Tyndale. "We haven't had a call from Master Belsey, yet you can gamble he's in Antwerp. Antwerp. Also a dozen more the likes of him."

(Belsey, we were soon to learn, was not in Antwerp—but in England.)

"Of the two dangers," I said, "he's the least. Lying here at the Adventurers' dock, we're safe. Belsey wouldn't dare touch us here."

"We'll go with the weather God gave us," Uncle Jack said. "We are embarked on His mission. He will still the winds. He will calm the waters. If need be, He will part the seas."

Tyndale, hearing my uncle's sanctimonious prediction, looked dubious.

"That's a mighty favor to ask—this parting of the seas," he said. "I'd much prefer that you set out on a more promising day. Your ship is a stout one, yet . . ."

"Stout as oak can make it," Uncle Jack broke in. "Stout a ship as ever sailed a watery sea. Built by a great builder, Jeremiah Barton."

He was speaking of my Grandfather Jeremiah, who was a shipwright and built ships on his farm under a shed at the edge of the bay.

A story is told about Grandfather Barton that everyone swore was true, and I believed it. He was walking along the shore one morning near where he was building a fishing boat when he heard low moans as from someone in distress. Stopping to listen, he saw nearby a young mermaid lying among the rocks with strands of seaweed clinging to her hair. Grandfather approached the beautiful mermaid and asked why she was moaning.

"The tide went out and left me here and I am slowly dying of thirst and the sun," said the mermaid. "If you will only put me back in the sea, then I'll grant you any wish your heart desires."

Grandfather, because he was a kind man and a good shipwright, said, "I wish to build strong ships that can go to sea and never sink and drown a single sailor." The beautiful mermaid agreed to the bargain, and Grandfather carried her back to the sea. Grandfather Jeremiah lived to be eighty years old, but the beautiful mermaid still kept her promise.

"A hundred ships he built," Uncle Jack said, "and never a sinking or a drowning. Not a sailor or a ship lost. Eh, Tom?"

"A great shipwright," I agreed. "But I don't think we should depend so much on Grandfather Jeremiah."

"We are not depending on him, Tom. We put our faith in God. It is He we depend upon."

Uncle Jack's dependence upon God was as variable as the weather.

The wind had grown sharper, the scudding clouds covered the sky. I feared that they were outriders of a storm. I had a chance to speak my mind further, to claim the ship as my own, to give the command that would delay our sailing. But I hesitated, was silent, was finally stared down.

Uncle Jack took his eyes from me and gave a final signal to the carpenter. The man crouched with his maul and drove home the last of the wedges.

Uncle Jack glanced at Tyndale. "Do you sail with us?" he asked pointedly. "We have a bunk for you and a good store of food."

Tyndale had told us already that he was bound for Marburg, after he had raised more money among the Adventurers for a printing of the Old Testament, which he yet had not translated. Uncle Jack's invitation was a polite request, therefore, for him to leave the ship before she sailed.

Tyndale said nothing, but it was not because his mind was undecided. He knew well that he could never go home to England. He had told me so before. It was in his eyes now as he looked up at the masts and the still-furled sails.

The wind and the blows of the carpenter's maul were the only sounds on deck.

"Do you sail with us?" Uncle Jack asked once more, not unkindly but impatient to be off.

In answer Tyndale backed away, climbed over the bulwarks, and scrambled to the dock.

"I'll take good care of your Bibles," I shouted down to him.

"And of yourself," he shouted back. "And your reading. I left a Bible in your bunk."

Sails began to fill and the lines were cast off. With wind and ebbing tide at her stern, the *Black Pearl* moved quickly into the stream.

Tyndale's hair flew out in the wind. He raised a hand and held it high above his head. I watched him standing there alone on the deserted dock with his hand raised, until a gust of rain swept him from view.

Chapter 22

The storm struck us when we were eight leagues northeast of Ramsgate, close upon the Sands.

We had sailed until nightfall with the wind astern, but near one in the morning the wind freshened and shifted to our starboard beam. At once the ship heeled hard to port, the shrouds hummed, and great dollops of gray water came aboard. The water sluiced down the deck. Too much for the scuppers, it piled up against the bulwarks and went roaring over the side.

Uncle Jack gave orders to reef, but not more than a handful of canvas came in, and we went on our way. He stood at the break of the roundhouse, where he had a forward view of the ship, shouting commands to our meager crew, sending me on errands fore and aft. He sent me everywhere except aloft. He ran my legs off. And he gave me no time to think about the storm or of anything else.

A black wave came crashing aboard, and suddenly we stood knee-deep in a tide of violent water.

"The Bibles," Uncle Jack shouted. "The Bibles."

I knew what he meant.

Snatching a light from the cabin, I sloshed across the deck, my sea boots filled with water, and stumbling headlong made my way down the companionway into the noisy darkness of the hold.

Here below, the sounds of the wind and crashing seas faded to a whisper. But there were other sounds—the planking creaked, cargo rustled as it shifted gently with the roll of the ship. It was like being on the inside of a drum.

I shone my lantern overhead along the oaken deck beams and knees. There was no sign of running water anywhere.

The books were stored in a secret place built by Grandfather Jeremiah. In our town of Danfield everyone was a smuggler. Indeed, our town was famous for miles around, all along the coasts of Essex and Kent, for its smuggling.

Grandfather Jeremiah had built the secret place for my father where the mainmast rested hard upon the keel. At this spot, around the butt of the mast, he built a compartment four feet high and seven feet square. It was timbered with heavy oak and made to look as if it supported the mast. But one side was fitted carefully, like the drawer of a cabinet, with wooden pins. When you removed them, one side of the compartment revealed the secret storing place.

I drew out the pins, let the heavy timber down, and shone the lantern inside. The compartment was dry and smelled of ink.

The barrels and packs were also dry and had not shifted. I put the timber back in place, once again shone the lantern along the planking overhead, and went on deck to report to Uncle Jack.

"She's dry as a bone," I told him.

Stiff with salt, his beard glittered in the lantern light.

"Praise the Lord," he shouted.

"And also Grandfather Jeremiah," I shouted back to him against the howl of the wind.

The wind slacked off toward morning though the seas still ran high. We took one roaring wave aboard that set us up on our beam ends, but the ship, with a long-drawn moan of hissing water and whistling cordage, the cries of long-dead sailors, shook it off and righted herself once more.

The day dawned clear and almost windless, with a pink horizon and one low cloud that followed us into the Medway.

We had planned to enter the river in the darkness before dawn, but the storm had sped us on. We had no choice except to sail clear of the mouth of the Thames, where we could expect to encounter a searcher.

Searchers seldom ventured as far up the Medway as the town of Danfield. They sometimes nosed around outside the entrance where the two rivers meet, but since the morning that one of them was seized, carried aboard by a fisherman, and deposited miles away on a lonely islet to find his way back to London as best he could, searchers mostly stayed off the Medway and out of the town of Danfield.

Our pier, with its crooked piling and ragged deck, had a broken-down look, which we encouraged so as to avert suspicion that it was ever used.

A winding, weed-grown path led to an old Roman watchtower. To further allay suspicion, we kept scythes, shears, plows, and a pile of harness in the tower. Under the pile of harness were heavy paving stones and under the stones was a stone trap door, which led by a winding stairs to a large storage room. Thither that night we brought Tyndale's Bibles.

Three nights later we loaded the crates and barrels of Bibles into a cart and started west on the long journey to London, leading two horses and a milk cow to give us the appearance of farmers on the way to market.

We traveled mostly by day and slept under the cart on straw we later fed to the horses. On the morning of the third day, having passed through the town of Greenwich, we were waved off the road by outriders on spangled horses carrying two immense gilded crosses. From the weed-choked ditch where we sought refuge, we crouched and watched the procession go by.

Behind the cross-bearers and six yeomen carrying pikes and other weapons came a mule, and astride it a fat little man who Uncle Jack said was Cardinal Wolsey.

"He rides the mule," my uncle said, "to show us simple folk that he is a simple man of simple wants. But notice, Tom, that his cloak has a fur collar and the mule is harnessed with gilded leather and gold chains. Gold chains! Fur on the man's collar! What do you make of that, eh?"

"I make out that he is a rich man.'

Uncle Jack snorted. "Richer than the King. Palaces everywhere. Here and there. Likely he's on his way now to one of them. And riding a mule. To fool us, eh?"

I started to count the reeves and courtiers and retainers, all mounted on fine horses, who followed the fat man on the gold-laden mule. Then I began to count the yeomen and soldiers, some riding, some marching. Then three varlets came by driving a flock of sheep and six oxen. Then four men passed carrying three dead, trussed-up deer. Then came a cart filled with crates of partridges and pheasants.

"He eats well," Uncle Jack said. "I am told he serves twenty courses at a dinner. And all on gold plates, mind you. Fine fare, eh?"

The procession stretched out for a mile and more—men and perfumed women—jewels flashing, banners cracking in the morning breeze, flutes squealing, drums beating.

I watched the procession go by, counting to myself. At six hundred and fifty-seven I grew tired and quit.

Uncle Jack said, "What's in the barrels and crates behind us here will put an end to all this. He's doomed, this Wolsey and his like. And Tyndale's Bible will have a big part in the dooming. Doomed, I tell you, Tom. And good riddance, eh?"

We got our cart out of the ditch and back on the high road and resumed the journey. As we jolted on our way toward London, the crates and barrels creaking behind us, I wondered about Uncle Jack's prophecy, doubting that it would ever come to pass.

Chapter 23

We reached London Bridge, as was our intent, at the busiest hour of the morning, when a mob on foot and a hundred carts were moving across the river from Southwark. There was nothing about us—horse, cart, or cargo—to attract attention.

Furthermore, the barrels and crates of goods were protected by a docket we had purchased at customs before we reached the bridge.

It had hurt Uncle Jack considerably to pay out good shillings for a piece of paper. But he comforted himself with the thought that when we sailed the ship into London he could use the docket, if need be, to cover the cargo still aboard.

Nonetheless, as we jostled and bullied our way across the bridge and proceeded at a sprightly pace toward our destination, we kept a weather eye out for Master Belsey and other searchers we knew by sight.

At St. Catherine's Way we ducked to the right and followed the creek in its windings until, close upon the river, we pulled up at the warehouse of Smith and Sons.

The warehouse was small and unprosperous-looking to the casual eye, but buried beneath it was half a mile of storage rooms, warrens, and tunnels. One of the tunnels, which ran down to the river bank, we had used many times in the past, discharging cargo there directly from the ship under cover of night.

We hastily unloaded our cargo, saw that it was properly hidden in the safest of the many warrens, paid the large storage fee for the privilege, and set off in our empty cart for St. Paul's.

Since the cathedral lay at a considerable distance, we stopped to buy fresh eggs from a vendor and had six of them coddled to our order and served with broiled herring at a quiet inn in Vanity Lane.

After breakfast Uncle Jack wiped his whiskers with the back of his fist, and let out his belt two full notches.

"Consider this," he said. "The successful labor of Herr Schoeffer in Worms. Your safe voyage down the Rhine. Our fortunate meeting in Antwerp. The storm withstood. Uneventful days on the road to London. A safe storing of our cargo. God favors our mission, eh, Tom?"

"He favors it so far," I said.

We sat on a bench before a crackling fire. The food had made me drowsy.

"So far? So far? You have doubts, eh?"

"I'll feel better," I said, rousing myself, "when the Bibles are out of the way. Remember that we still have a thousand of them to deliver."

"You can do that easy enough. You've a way about you, Tom. A way. Like your Grandfather Jeremiah, who could charm a partridge out of a tree."

"You don't plan to help me," I said, seeing through his flattery.

"I'd be in the way. Cause suspicions. My whiskers and all. Apt to scare right-thinking people, eh?"

There was some truth in what Uncle Jack said. He did indeed have about him a shaggy, piratical, unpromising look that might cause distrust.

"I can sell a thousand Bibles," I said. "But what about the four thousand still sitting over there in Antwerp?"

"We'll need to bring them to England and store them in different places along the coast until we can find good markets. Think of the profits, Tom. We'll be rich as dukes, eh?"

"What if the ship is seized," I said, "and she has a thousand heretical books in her hold? What do we say? What do we do then? We can't get off by paying a fine."

"We go to prison," said Uncle Jack in a matter-of-fact tone. "One of His Majesty's more comfortable prisons."

"He has none," I said. "None that you could call comfortable."

"In a short time we'll pay our way out."

"With our necks?"

"With good hard gold."

I thought for a while, then decided that this was the time to broach the subject of the ship's ownership.

"It comes back to the *Black Pearl*," I said. "She was built by my grandfather. She was owned by my father. Upon his death it was passed on to you. But still I have an interest in her."

Uncle Jack gave me a long glance.

"Interest. Pride. Tradition. You have them all," he said. "They're in your bones. Fine things to have, eh?"

"But it's more than pride I'm talking about, Uncle Jack. I wish a rightful share in the ship and its profits."

"Not a coxswain's pay," I continued, "but a rightful share."

Of a sudden Uncle Jack grew serious. His eyes, glowing with the light of the renewed fire, fixed themselves upon me in a steady, calculated gaze.

"I've promised oft before that I'd give you a share of the business . . ."

"On several occasions," I said.

"And it's my intention to honor that promise. I am an honorable man, Tom boy, never one to weasel on his word. You are young. Very young. In a year's time, when you've gained knowledge of seamanship and money matters, that'll be the occasion for a pact between us, uncle and nephew like. And you'll find Uncle Jack a generous man in matters of money. As well you know. Generous to a fault, I've been told."

"I've always wondered," I said, keeping my strong feelings in check, "about my father's passing the *Black Pearl* on to you. There was no reason for him not to leave the ship to me."

"None that I know of, Tom. But that's what he did—keel and keelson, masts and sails. Left her all to me. I think that he intended that it be yours, half yours, one day. And that's what I intend. Not that he ever said so much. But that was my feeling. And that's what I'll do, as I've said. Give you a proper share when, man and sailor, you're ready."

"There never was a deed, was there, Uncle Jack? A will my father made?"

"None that I ever saw, Tom. None that I ever heard of. None."

A pair of sailors from the *Mary Rose* lounged in and stood in front of the blazing fire, warming their seats. Seeing the chance to put an end to our conversation, Uncle Jack called out to them, recalling the day the previous year when the *Mary*

Rose had escorted us out of the harbor at Gravesend. I got up, and as I passed him on the way out, I whispered a caution.

"Remember William Roye and Cologne," I warned him.

He waved a hand in reply and gave me a wink, but I doubted that he would keep his tongue in check.

In the empty cart I drove straight to St. Paul's and began transactions for the sale of our thousand Bibles.

The booksellers who had bought the Luther pamphlets had been jailed for selling them. Three other booksellers, whose names Tyndale had given me, I managed to get in touch with and after two days of transaction sold and delivered all the Bibles, but at less of a profit than we had hoped for. Nevertheless, Uncle Jack had a bag of gold in his coat, and in high good spirits we set forth across London Bridge.

The tide was running strong, causing a mighty uproar as it rushed against the starlings on its way to the sea. The bells of the city were striking the hour of two, but they sounded faint against the thunderous racing of the tide.

London was covered with a pearly mist, yet here and there lights began to shine. Uncle Jack stopped the cart, and we sat looking back upon the sight, the wonderful city of London.

"The Bibles will all be sold," he said. "The faithful will read them and read them and London will never again be as it is now. And we'll be rich as dukes."

At Deptford, a short distance below London, we managed to hail a horse barge and driving aboard made the rest of the journey by water, thereby arriving at the Medway before nightfall.

We felt pleased with ourselves as we drove away from the landing on the short road to home. The smoke from the evening fire of Danfield showed gray against a pink sky. The black, gold-laced hull of the *Black Pearl,* calmly riding at anchor, caught the last of the sun.

Uncle Jack hefted the gold and passed it over for me to heft, then took it back and put it away in his coat.

"What do you think about the four thousand Bibles still in Antwerp? What's your thought, eh?"

"We'll talk about them when we get home," I said firmly. "And of other matters, too," I said to myself.

Chapter 24

The sun had set as I opened the gate and Uncle Jack drove into the yard, unharnessed the horse, and let it loose.

A warm light was shining through the front window, and there was a good smell of meat roasting in the fireplace. Our housekeeper, Millie, was a fine cook, having won prizes at the fair for her pigeon pies. I certainly liked her cooking better than what you get in London. My mouth was watering when I opened the door, thinking of the good things Millie was cooking for supper.

Millie was standing with her back to the fireplace, her hands clasped in front of her, an odd position, I thought, for her hands were always busy at something. She was staring at me, which was strange, too.

Then I saw off to one side, not five steps away, a man planted solid as a tree, with his feet apart and a pistol pointed in my direction. Coming out of the dark into the light, I failed to recognize him at first, until he spoke, and then I knew that it was Herbert Belsey, the searcher.

Uncle Jack was still outside, bedding down the horse. He could have made a run for it and escaped had it not been for three armed men who were hiding in the barn. They put a knife at his throat and marched him into the kitchen.

"What's this about? An outrage. Outrage," Uncle Jack shouted, glaring around.

"We'll explain that later when you have more time," Herbert Belsey said, giving him a flat stare. "Get your clothes together and all your money. You'll need both where you're going."

"An outrage," Uncle Jack shouted again. "A man not safe in his own home. Outrage. The sheriff. Where's the sheriff?"

"We have a flood tide," Belsey said, not raising his voice. "We plan to make it."

There was a loaded musket hanging above the fireplace. Uncle Jack was too far away to get his hands on it, but all Millie needed to do was reach up and in one movement pull the trigger. A shot would alert the village. Everyone knew the

signal, having heard it before. Every villager would grab a weapon and come running.

Uncle Jack gave Millie a clear signal, but she missed it. She looked at him, puzzled, and stood by the fire wringing her hands.

None of the armed officers was bothering with me, probably because of my youth, my pink-cheeked look of innocence. I edged toward the fireplace, stopped to turn down a lamp that was beginning to smoke, then moved on to the fireplace and stood beside Millie, within reach of the loaded musket.

"Move," Belsey said to Uncle Jack.

Thereupon three of the officers prodded him with steel-tipped staffs. Two others brandished their swords.

Now was the time for me to act, to sound the alarm that would bring the villagers like a swarm of hornets down upon Belsey and his gang.

I turned and quickly reached for the musket. I even had a finger on the trigger. But by a second, by a split second, I was not quick enough. A steel-tipped spike caught me on the forearm, a blow that brought a choking pain to my throat. I staggered back and fell to the hearth.

"Up," an officer said quietly, prodding me with the sharp point of his sword. "Move, both of you. The tide's not waiting."

Uncle Jack pulled himself up to his full height, which meant that he had to check his head to keep from bumping the beams.

"Do you know that you are addressing the owner of the ship *Black Pearl?* A ship of considerable value. Registered in the King's books. A legitimate trader on the King's highways. Upon the seas of the world. Do you understand what I say, eh? Do you comprehend the consequences of your outrageous behavior? Outrageous, I say."

Belsey appeared to listen, but his eyes moved slowly around the room as if he were counting the value of each item—tables, chair, chests, rug, everything. When Uncle Jack had finished, Belsey said, "You speak of yourself as the owner of the ship *Black Pearl.* Did I hear you aright?"

Uncle Jack did not hesitate, though he well might have. "You hear aright. The owner. The legal owner."

The men brandished their weapons. If Uncle Jack had held a sword in his hand, he could have cleared the whole room of Belsey and his men. It was too late now to sound an alarm and bring the townspeople running. Yet there was one last hope.

Millie had a piercing call that could bring cows in from a mile away. In fact, she had won a prize once at the fair for her cow-calling. Alas, too frightened to scream, too scared even to speak, she stood in front of the fireplace still wringing her hands.

Belsey had a whip in his hand, and he gave Uncle Jack a clout with it. The five officers, staffs and swords in hand, shoved us through the door, down the dock, up the gangplank, and onto the ship.

Dogs began to bark in the village, not a quarter mile away, and for a moment I had hopes that they would start an alarm, but the barking ceased of a sudden.

The officers cast off the lines, and we drifted out into the stream, heading southward toward its meeting with the Thames. Only then, as we began to move downstream, did Millie come alive. She came running out of the house, skirts flying and hands raised to heaven, giving forth at the top of her lungs her prize-winning cow-call.

Doors were flung open in the village, and lights shone suddenly across the river. Dogs began to bark again. Men were running. A musket went off. Millie continued to scream. But by now the ship had moved away from the dock and was gaining speed.

We rounded a bend, met the back current of the Thames, were caught by the incoming tide, whirled about, and headed upstream in a surging rush toward London.

Uncle Jack and I were herded into what once had been his cabin, bound hand and foot, and left there on the floor.

"What happened to the gold?" I whispered to him when things had quieted down outside.

"Tossed it in the bushes," he whispered back. "Millie will find it before the night's out. Millie's good at finding things."

"We'll need it in London."

"That and more. Greedy palms there in London. And a lot of them. Searchers watched by other searchers who in turn are watched by other searchers. Three different sets of searchers, spying on each other. All at once. All with their hands out. Dogs eating dogs, eh?"

"We're carrying no contraband," Uncle Jack went on. "No corn. No wool. No iron. No leather. Nothing. And we've a pink ticket to prove it. Nothing. Clean as a whistle, we are. And every last Bible sold and delivered."

A creaking boot stopped at the door. I gave Uncle Jack a warning look, and we both fell silent.

I lay there on the cabin floor, in pain from the ropes that bound me, but still the pain was mild against an overpowering fear. We were, as Uncle Jack had said, clean as a whistle, with a docket to prove it.

"It puzzles my thoughts," Uncle Jack whispered. "Just three weeks ago the office of the surveyor of customs dared not risk a surprise check on his books, so after dark he sent his servant to climb in the window and steal the documents. Time being short and no chance to alter the records, the surveyor thereupon made a bonfire of the lot. A big fire. Burned up most of the records. Burned most of the office."

"What's that to do with us?" I asked.

"Plenty enough," Uncle Jack said. "The only records they have against me, against us, were burned up in that bonfire. Most of them, at least."

As I lay there, bound hand and foot, thinking hard about our plight, Uncle Jack's story somehow did not reassure me.

Chapter 25

We reached London Bridge before the tide turned and, in the dark, moored off the customs dock.

There was some discussion on deck, which we faintly heard, about taking us ashore, but it was finally decided, because of the recent fire, to leave us where we lay until morning. Our hands were untied, and we were each given a bowl of cold gruel to eat. Then, our hands tied again, we were left for the night, with a guard posted beside the cabin door.

At dawn my feet were unbound, and I was rowed ashore and marched into customs, what was left of it, one large room smelling of smoke, cold and bare except for a bench and a barred window that looked out upon the river. From the window I could see our ship riding trimly at anchor and two guards lounging against the roundhouse, from time to time arousing themselves long enough to spit upon the deck.

I waited until noon, when I was given another bowl of thin soup, this time with small pieces of eel floating about. I sat there for hours, until the room darkened and long streamers of failing light fell across the Thames.

Then a door opened and a light shone in my eyes. It was Herbert Belsey carrying a lantern but no weapons, not even his whip. However, as I looked him full in the face, so upturned was his nose that I felt now as I always felt, that his nostrils were the two black barrels of a pistol pointed squarely at my head.

He smiled a twisted but plausible smile that, considering everything, surprised me. He put the lantern on the floor, which was covered with musty month-old straw, and sat down on the bench facing me.

"I'll not take up time apologizing for the treatment you have recently undergone," he said.

"Am undergoing," I corrected him. "At the moment. Yesterday and today."

"Because I lack the time or the inclination for courtesies," he said. "Let us proceed. I've talked to you before, in Cologne if you remember, about the ownership of the *Black Pearl.* I explained then, and I repeat once more that you are the ship's sole and rightful owner. You were unconvinced then about the matter of ownership. Are you still unconvinced?"

"Yes, sir. I doubt that my uncle would lie to me. I see no reason for him to do so."

Belsey reached deep into an inner pocket and drew forth a legal-looking document bound with a ribbon, which he untied, and thrust the whole before me.

"Can you read?" he asked. "If not I'll read it to you."

Angered somewhat that he considered me an ignorant bumpkin, I took the document without a word, walked over to the barred window where the light was better, and read it aloud in a firm voice, though I did stumble over several words I had never seen before.

"You read all right," Belsey conceded. "Now tell me, do you understand what you've read? Does it make sense to you?"

He thrust his head toward me in a long stare. In the lantern light the scar on his face did not seem so disfiguring as I remembered it when I had first seen it in Cologne, months before.

"Do you understand what you've read?" he asked again.

"A manifest. A ship's manifest," I answered.

"A list of goods, some twenty in all, listed in detail by your uncle, Jack Barton. Put down item by item and at the end signed with his signature. Have you seen the manifest before?"

"I don't remember it."

"Do you recognize the writing and the signature? Do they belong to your uncle?"

"It looks like his writing."

"Is it, I ask you, his handwriting? Surely you recognize your uncle's signature."

I kept my silence, whereupon Belsey reached into his capacious cloak and pulled forth a second document. It was more legal in appearance than the first, on finer paper, and tied with a ribbon. He spread it out on the bench where the full glow of the lantern fell upon it.

"Now read carefully," Belsey said. "Pay close attention to the handwriting and to the signature."

I did as I was directed, and when I had finished, Belsey placed the first document, the list of imported items, down beside it.

"Now note," he said, holding the lantern above the two papers, "and you'll see that the first item filed with us at customs is a list of goods imported from Hamburg, upon which duty was paid."

I recognized the paper instantly, remembering well the goods declared, an excellent ship's mast for one thing, and the date. And Uncle Jack's crabbed, chicken-track signature. I also recalled the goods we had not declared—a bale of fine goat's hair, for instance.

"Do you recognize this manifest?" Belsey asked.

"I've seen it before," I answered.

"Now compare this list with the writing in the document beside it, which purports to be your father's last will and testament, in which he bequeaths his ship, the *Trident,* to your uncle, Jack Barton."

I read the document slowly, aware before I had finished the first sentence that it was a forgery, a poor imitation of my father's handwriting.

"Did the same man write both documents?" Belsey asked in the tones of a magistrate badgering a witness.

"I don't know."

"Certainly you're familiar with your uncle's writing."

"Not very familiar."

"He's written you a letter? A note?"

"Yes. Two or three."

"You don't remember the handwriting?"

"Not well."

"Do the two documents look as if they were written by the same hand? Do the *T*'s look the same? The *S*'s? The signature?"

"I haven't a good eye for these matters," I said.

I walked over to the barred window and looked out, thinking fast. I didn't want to get mixed up with Belsey in the ownership of the boat, but I was in trouble. There was no question that Uncle Jack had destroyed my father's will, if he had ever written one, and substituted a will of his own.

The ship by law belonged to me. That was clear. Belsey knew it, and I knew it.

Through the window I could see the *Black Pearl* riding calmly on the tide but showing no lights except a dim glow in the master's cabin, where, I assumed, Uncle Jack was still bound and guarded.

"There's no riding light on the ship," I said to Belsey. "The river's full of traffic. Without a riding light she could be hit or sunk. Something should be done about her at once. She's a hazard, lying there in the night, a dark dangerous hull."

"Come," Belsey said, seizing me by the arm. "We'll hang a light on her."

The two of us rowed out the short distance to the ship and lighted her riding lantern. As I went by the Master's cabin, I peered in and, seeing no one, asked Belsey what had become of my uncle.

"He's in safe hands. He'll not bother you."

"I didn't think that he would bother me."

"Begging your pardon, uncle or not, he's a forger and a cutthroat," Belsey said. "And the sooner you realize the same, the better for you."

"Where is he?" I asked again.

"In Clink."

Clink was the most notorious of London's many prisons, just across the river from customs, filthy, rat-infested, and difficult to grease your way out of unless you had a small fortune to pass around.

I was still not satisfied that Belsey had removed Uncle Jack from the ship and I took a look around, giving the excuse that I wanted to see that everything was shipshape. Belsey followed me with a proprietary air, as if he were a part-owner already, over the deck, into the galley, the hold, the bilge.

If Uncle Jack was still aboard, the two of us could overpower Belsey, haul anchor, and in five minutes, the tide apace with us, be halfway down the river on our way out of the country. But he was apparently nowhere within hailing distance.

Belsey took me back to the room that smelled of smoke and told me to make a bed for myself in the straw. He went to the door, opened it, closed it again, and as a sort of afterthought came back and put the lantern down and hoisted his foot up on the bench.

"I could send you over to Clink," he said, "along with your dear uncle. But I have a suggestion. Perhaps an idea that will appeal to you more than residence in prison. I alluded to it once before, in Cologne, when I had learned that the ship belonged to you and not to your uncle. Do you recall the occasion?"

"Something of what was said. Not much."

"This is it. You own the *Black Pearl*. Your rights to it will not be contested in court. Herbert Belsey, Esquire, will see to that. Nor will it be questioned by your uncle. He'll reside in Clink for a year or two at the least, perhaps longer should we find it necessary. Your rights will not be contested because of me. Your uncle will reside in prison until I see fit to free him. For this service—and I presume we can give it this term— for this service I demand a half interest in the *Black Pearl*. A partnership. Share and share alike. You to handle the ship. Go where you will. Buy what you wish. Bring your goods into London at will. No fees, no duties. In five years' time, if all goes well, if the *Book of Rates* is not changed, if the searchers are taken care of decently, we'll both be gentlemen of property."

He picked up his lantern and went to the door.

As he stood there, I walked toward him, considering my chances of catching him unawares, of overpowering him, of making my way under cover of darkness to the ship. The anchor was heavy, but I could handle it. Once free, the ship would catch the tide.

It was the first time in my life I had considered an action without thinking of Uncle Jack, without calling upon him in spirit, without depending upon his advice or presence. It gave me sudden strength to realize that I was now on my own, my own man, no longer dependent upon anyone in the world except myself.

Voices beyond the door brought me to a halt. I was within a step of Belsey. I could have reached out and taken him by the throat. Wisely, I backed away and bowed stiffly, as he said, "There's no hurry, Master Barton. Take time to consider. If you should decide not to entertain my offer, we can declare the ship King's property by default and you will thereby be relieved of all responsibilities."

He closed the door and barred it. I crossed the room and for a long time stood at the window. The tide was at ebb, and the roar through the arches of London Bridge had not begun.

In the quiet, cries and moans and then shouts came across the water from Clink. I wondered if Uncle Jack lent his voice to the uproar.

Then it was quiet again. The tide turned, and the water rushed under the bridge on its way to the sea, drowning out all sounds of pain and anger. The *Black Pearl* strained at her anchor, as if anxious to slip her moorage, to flee down the river to the open sea.

I stood at the barred window and looked out upon the dark river stitched with the lights of passing barges.

There was a glow on the far bank and against it I saw, or thought I saw, a figure standing, a man with arm upraised, not beckoning, just a lone figure standing there in the night who disappeared as I saw him. But in that moment it was clear to me what my answer to Belsey would be, as clear as if it were written in letters of fire on the flowing stream.

Chapter 26

In midmorning Belsey came to the door and, guessing rightly that I had decided to agree to his offer or at the least to consider it, invited me out to eat.

We walked some distance to an inn not far from St. Paul's, and there he ordered me a breakfast fit for an earl—herring and quail eggs and a hot partridge pie—though eating sparsely himself.

While I devoured my food, not having eaten properly for nigh on to two days, he talked some about the weather, much about the harbors of Amsterdam and Antwerp—testing my knowledge, I presume—and at last about my familiarity with the New World, of which there was considerable talk of late.

I finished my partridge pie and could have eaten another if it would not have appeared unseemly. As a matter of fact, Belsey asked me to have a second helping, which, for appearance' sake, I reluctantly refused.

"What are the dimensions of the *Black Pearl?*" he asked.

"Sixty feet overall, twenty-five feet in the beam, and of a hundred tuns burden." (For those not nautical, this meant that the ship could carry one hundred double hogsheads of wine or their equivalent in weight.)

"Not a big one," Belsey said.

"As big as the ships of Christopher Columbus. His *Santa María* and *Niña.* And a sturdier ship by far than either."

Belsey asked for ink and quill and when they were at hand, made a series of notations in a small book he carried in his cuff. In the meantime I ate a delicious cake that the girl had brought me, apparently thinking from my wan looks that I was in need of it.

"What are your thoughts on the spice trade?" Belsey asked. "I hear that it's a profitable one, gaining every day in popularity. Spices are being used in lady's perfume, as well as to enhance the flavor of English mutton, which often has a moldy taste. And fish that is not quite fresh, it greatly assists."

"Unfortunately," I said, aware that I was fast getting in over my head, "unfortunately, the Portuguese have a monopoly on the trade."

Belsey made another notation, then looked up and gave me one of his long, flat stares. "There's good money in slaves," he said. "How many could you contrive to carry on a voyage, say, of six weeks from Hispaniola to London?"

"I've never given it thought," I said.

"If you were to give it thought, what would be your estimate? Fifty, sixty? Twenty women, forty men? Would that be a fair guess?"

"Close enough," I said.

"They can be crowded into small space," Belsey said. "Sleep on deck in all weather. Very hardy people, I'm told. And also eat little except fruit."

"But they don't do well in cold climes," I said. "Ships arrive in Spain with more than half the people dying. One caravel lost ninety-three of them. Saved only one: a child of five."

Belsey was still making notes in his little book, pulling it out of his cuff, scribbling in it, closing it, and putting it back in a businesslike way.

I did not bother to tell him that I would never captain a ship that carried slaves either as cargo or as impressed sailors. My father had not done so. Uncle Jack had not done so. Nor would I. Nor did I tell him that my last wish in the world would be to work with him as a partner, in any capacity or on any voyage I could think of.

He was not long in coming to the point. Having tested my knowledge of ships—rifled my sea bag, so to speak—induced me into a good mood, or so he thought, by partridge pie, he presented his proposition bluntly.

We had reached Charing Cross on our way back to the customs office and were waiting for a line of carts to pass when he said, "We can form a partnership, hold between us sixty percent of the company, and dispose of the rest at a handsome profit."

"But I don't own the ship," I said, darting between carts. Of a more cautious nature, Belsey waited for a better opening. When he caught up with me, I continued, "Should I come into ownership, why should I present you with thirty percent of the same?"

"Because," said Belsey without a moment's hesitation, "and I've already explained this to you, unless I do share in the ownership, the boat will be confiscated and turned over to the King's Exchequer."

"You have the power to do that?"

"It's not a matter of power, young man. If the ship doesn't belong to Jack Barton or to Tom Barton, then it belongs for the moment to no one. Now if this ship that belongs to no one happens to be suspected of smuggling goods in and out of the London port for two years and more—and its unlawful activities can be proven by depositions from merchants who have received smuggled goods—then the ship is subject to seizure. Do I make myself clear?"

We had reached the room where I had spent the night. Belsey opened the door and stepped aside for me to enter. The smell of smoke and musty straw assailed my throat.

"Why am I being kept here? What law have I broken?" I asked.

"You are a smuggler," Belsey said.

"So is everyone else. There's not a ship that goes in and out of London that doesn't carry smuggled goods."

"True," said Belsey. "But some smugglers we catch."

He closed the door and opened it again, thrusting his head in to say, "You can have a barrister if you wish. Shall I send you one? He may be able to have you sent to Clink. To keep your uncle company. I would agree for you to go there should you wish. It's easy to get in but difficult to get out." He started to close the door, paused, and said, "By the way, have you seen William Tyndale of late? No? Well, neither have I. But I'm hopeful."

Belsey didn't send me a barrister, but in less than a minute he brought in a young man who meanwhile must have been waiting in the corridor.

He was tall and handsome, with a full beard, curled hair, and a jeweled dagger at his belt. I had the feeling that I had seen him before. I was certain that our paths had crossed at some time, if only momentarily. I had the impression that he had the same thoughts about me.

"My name is Henry Phillips," he announced at the same moment Belsey introduced him. "I'm familiar with your name. It's highly thought of on the river and in the Lowlands."

"Mr. Phillips is furnishing the money for our enterprises," Belsey said. "And in consideration thereof will own an interest in the New World Exploration and Trading Company."

"It has a name already?" I said, somewhat taken aback.

With grave misgivings, flanked on one side by Herbert Belsey, on the other by Henry Phillips, and behind by two gentlemen dressed in finery and with the air of being high-born, I signed the document Phillips now laid before me. We all signed it, one after the other, then crossed the street and celebrated the signing.

Before I had finished my meal, I had made up my mind that my first voyage would be not to the New World but to the warehouse in Antwerp where Tyndale's Bibles were stored.

And my first act now that I was a free man would be to cross the river and learn what had become of my Uncle Jack.

Chapter 27

There were many fires in London. There seemed to be one going on at every moment, day and night.

Strange, therefore, that the one fire that should have taken place and did not was the burning down from cellar to garret of the filthiest collection of verminous halls, rat-infested rooms, refuse-laden courtyards in all of the city of London. On a dark night in the deepest fog, when you could not see your hand in front of you, you could find your way to Clink by simply following your nose.

And this is exactly what I did the night I went off to visit Uncle Jack. I crossed to Southwark with the smell in my nostrils. I walked down the embankment guided by the ever-increasing stench and came to the narrow entrance on Clink Street without making a wrong turn, asking directions, or so much as taking an extra step. If you had a cold and your nose failed, the hubbub would have sufficed to guide you.

Clink was not the prison where Uncle Jack, according to the laws he had broken, should have resided. It was maintained for the city's riffraff, failed owlers, dregs of the waterfront, even castoffs from Blackfriars up the river where there were no laws and London's criminals were safe from sheriffs, magistrates, or even the King's henchmen. It was London's human garbage dump, and it took pride in its reputation.

I arrived there in the early evening, dressed in the new clothes bought by funds the New World Exploration and Trading Company had advanced.

Belsey, of course, had no interest in my visit to Clink, for it was his hope to keep Uncle Jack locked up there until the ship's papers were properly transferred, and as long thereafter as possible.

I was forewarned by friends that I was to ask for and if possible talk only to Samuel Carswell, chief warden of Clink, Mr. Carswell being a man of wide connection and great power. In this I was unsuccessful.

From the street, I entered a noisome corridor, dark as a dungeon and smelling of rats, windowless, slippery underfoot. I came to a small room furnished with a low counter, a large ledger, ink and quill, and a scruffy old woman in a scarlet wrapper.

"What do ye wish?" she asked in a sweet-toned, little girl's voice. "Anything I can help you with, sir?"

"I am looking for Master Samuel Carswell."

"What's your name?"

"Tom Barton."

"And occupation."

"I'm with the New World Exploration and Trading Company."

"In what capacity?" she asked, examining me from head to foot with a faded but practiced eye.

"As an officer."

"Master Carswell is not in at the present," she said sweetly. "I look for him tomorrow or the day following. If you leave your name, I will attempt to arrange a meeting. But meanwhile may I ask the purpose of your visit? Perhaps someone else can be of help."

"Perhaps you can help me," I said, dropping on the counter a bright coin. "I wish to talk to Jack Barton."

The sound had a solid ring to it that caused a startling change in the old woman. She immediately opened the ledger and began to read names, muttering them to herself, wetting her thumb as she turned each page. "Bills, Ball, Bing, Barks, Banton." She went on and on, then looked up and said, "Barton. Jack Barton?"

"That's the man. Jack Barton."

"Aged twenty-seven years. Native of Danfield. Charged with smuggling. Right, sir?"

"Right. But Clink is an odd place to hold a man on a charge of smuggling."

"Other places are cram-full. You take what you get these days and don't complain. Besides, there're worse ones than Clink." She closed the ledger with a bang. "Wait here, sir."

I waited for the better part of an hour, and the room filled up before she came back with a long-faced young man in tow. He carried a bundle of keys and motioned me to follow him.

We went up three flights of stairs, from a first floor where there seemed to be some order and an effort at cleanliness. But on the second floor it was all confusion: rooms without panes, the holes stuffed with paper and rags, straw pallets a dozen to the room. The next flight up, the third floor, contained no chairs, tables, or pallets. Inhabitants of these quarters were strewn here and about, as if swept there by a broom.

In one of these rooms, high up against a gable with a broken and boarded-up window, I found Uncle Jack.

His ankles were chained, and the chains fastened to an iron staple driven into a floor beam. There were five other men in the room, all of them gaunt-faced and the color of the refuse that surrounded them.

Uncle Jack, before he spoke to me, signaled that I should give the long-faced young man a coin, which I did, at the same time informing him that if he could find a better room there would be other coins forthcoming.

The youth looked me up and down insolently, apparently deemed me worth another coin, disappeared, and before Uncle Jack and I had exchanged a dozen words was back. He unlocked the leg chains and led us down one flight of decaying stairs to the second floor, and there held out his hand for the promised coin.

Here the room was larger. There was a pane in the one window, a small brick oven in the center of the floor where food could be cooked. Three straw pallets lay against one side of the room, all of them occupied by men who seemed to be sick; at least they were rolling about and groaning.

"Money doesn't talk here in Clink. It shouts. It screams," Uncle Jack said, motioning me to sit on the floor, there being no other place to sit. "Without money you die of disease or starvation. You pay for every morsel you put in your mouth. The rich who dwell on the first floor send out and have their viands brought in. Here we scrounge and steal and live on refuse unfit for animals. Unfit. An outrage. You must arrange to bring in food until I can pay my way out. Which will be soon. What has happened to the bag of gold coins, eh? The bag I tossed in the bushes by the barn, beside the old boiler. In the weeds. Look for it. Millie may have found it already. Bring it. Without fail. Tomorrow, eh?"

"Not tomorrow. I can't make the trip in that time."

"Soon then. The next day. Do not tarry and do not come back without it." He paused and thought for a moment. "The ship. We can get a loan on the ship. If all else fails, eh?"

I said nothing about the ship nor of Belsey nor of the trading company, it being the worst of times to impart this information. I intended to give Uncle Jack half my interest in the new company, but this was not the time to say so. The problem now was to get my hands on enough money to buy his release. How much would be needed, I had no way of knowing.

From the prison I went to see Belsey, told him that I was taking the ship downriver for repairs, and with the tide sailed into the Medway before nightfall.

In the failing light and then by lantern I looked for the bag of coins Uncle Jack had tossed into the weeds. I scoured the bushes, the barns. I searched through the house. To make matters worse, Millie was not home. It took me until next morning to learn from townspeople that she had gone off with Jason Toller, the innkeeper, bragging to everyone that she had found a bag of coins and was rich as a countess.

Uncle Jack took the news of the lost coins and the absconding Millie without comment, being too angry for words, and was but mildly placated by six pork pies and two apple coddlings I managed to get to him through the long-faced keeper of the keys.

It was clear from talks, which I finally arranged with Samuel Carswell, that no amount of money would free Uncle Jack until six months had passed.

"This does not mean," said Mr. Carswell, an amiable, well-fed gentleman who looked as if, were he pricked with a bodkin, he would ooze money instead of blood, "that your uncle's condition cannot be greatly enhanced in the matter of food and clothing, of proper heat in winter, and a cool river breeze in summer. This can all be arranged. Come to me at any time with your creature requests; my door is always open and my heart likewise. After six months, perhaps in less time, the larger matter of his release can be discussed as well."

I thanked Mr. Carswell by leaving a pound note on his desk and went at once to a grocer directly across the street from the Anchor and Chain and arranged for them to supply Uncle Jack with food. I paid them half in advance and promised them the rest when I returned from a short voyage to Antwerp.

I next convinced Belsey that the ship needed a new mainmast and that it was available only in the Lowlands. Obligingly, he arranged for a cargo of seed corn, whose export was forbidden since there was a severe shortage in England. We had it loaded an hour before I sailed at dawn.

Belsey sat in his wherry, an oar in each hand, as the anchor came in.

"How long will it take to step the mast?" he asked.

"I'll not have it stepped," I called down to him. "They do a better job of it here."

"Cheaper?"

"No. Masts are one thing you don't skimp on."

"A new mast should put everything in shape."

We were moving away from Belsey, who was sitting idly in his wherry, computing the cost of a new mast.

"This is January," I said. "We can't set out for the Indies before the winter storms are over. Not before April."

Belsey began to row to keep up with us, but, catching a crab with every stroke, fell astern.

"Stay clear of Tyndale," he shouted. "Shun him like the plague."

Taking in the final length of anchor chain, I pretended not to hear him.

BOOK FOUR

Chapter 28

William Tyndale, to my surprise and great delight, I found on the very day we docked in Antwerp.

Indeed, sighting us from afar, he was at the pier to greet the ship, standing where I had seen him last, his hand upraised as if only a moment and not a month had gone by, as if it were all a single gesture of hail and farewell that had endured during the time I had been away.

"How's your grammar? The reading?" were the first words he spoke as I leaped from the ship and embraced him.

"Good," I shouted. "Good. I've signed a legal document and read every word. Almost every word. And signed my name, too. Here."

I reached into my doublet and pulled for the contract and proudly presented it, expecting him to read it at that moment, there on the dock. Instead, he remarked that he would read it later. What a keen disappointment this was to me, for I had looked ahead for days to his commendation.

"The Bibles are safe in London," I said, presuming that they were uppermost in his thoughts and therefore the news he was waiting to hear.

"I heard this from a Dutch captain only yesterday," he said. "The first word and it was wonderful to hear." He threw his arms around me and said, "Thank you, son. You've done much."

He had never used the word "son" before, and I was astonished to hear it. Pleased, too.

"I likewise hear that the book sells," he said.

"It sells, and they ask for more. The booksellers ask. People ask."

A bitter, gray wind was blowing down the channel straight out of the North Sea. It was too cold to take a deep breath, and I suggested that we go to my cabin, where I had a good coal fire burning.

"This is Monday, and on this day I go through the streets along the dock," Tyndale said. "The people here are very poor, and I help them if I can. I can go tomorrow, but this is the day I usually go. This is the day they look for me."

He didn't ask me to go with him and, to be truthful, I didn't want to. It was bitter cold. I had contraband cargo to unload and sell. I was thinking about the contract in my pocket and anxious to talk to him and to friends about it.

I hung back, but in the end, in a bad humor, I followed him along the dock and into an ice-rutted lane. There were no houses on the lane, only hovels fastened together, one against the other, like a colony of gray barnacles.

The street had a name that meant Fishtail Row in English. Only fishermen lived there, but no one had fished for weeks because of the storms. It smelled like Clink, and the people were also gray-looking from hunger, but they could move around and share their misery. They seemed happier than the people in Clink Prison, but not much.

Tyndale carried small packets of food in his cloak and passed them out where he thought they were the most needed, mostly among widows whose husbands had been drowned. He had a bag filled with small coins, and these he passed out to children. When the packets and the coins were gone, he stopped to talk, saying words of encouragement where he thought they might help, sometimes not talking at all but just sitting in silence as a partner and sharer of misery.

We spent the whole day on Fishtail Row, were present at two funerals, and saw a baby who had been born three days before and was not much larger than my fist; its mother had no milk to feed it. At nightfall we went the short way to the English Adventurers' quarters. There a big pine fire was burning, and everyone was happily red-faced and merry.

We found a snug corner where we could talk without being overheard. (The English Adventurers were strongly Lutheran in their sympathies, as strong as the Hanseatic merchants at the Steelyard in London, but it was not wise to trust potboys, varlets, and others who could be bribed to repeat a word or a whisper they had picked up.) Besides this danger there were a number of spies in Antwerp, some employed by King Henry and others by Thomas More—all of them, to a man, anxious to get their hands on Tyndale and haul him back to England to face trial as a heretic.

Tyndale was safe with the Merchant Adventurers Company, on the docks surrounding its warehouse, and on Fishtail Row. Everywhere else in the cities of Rotterdam, Antwerp, and Amsterdam his life was in danger.

We ate, which helped to remove some of the chill from our bones, and I again brought forth my contract with the New World Exploration and Trading Company. Tyndale's gaze fell at once upon the name Herbert Belsey.

"By Satan's muddy bones!" he exclaimed. "However did you make connections with Belsey?"

"By circumstances. The last thing I would do otherwise."

I had expected Tyndale's criticism and was ready for it. I explained everything from the day I learned that I was the owner of the ship. I told him about the night we were caught by Belsey and his gang. I told him how we had been held in chains, how the ship had been threatened with seizure, everything until the signing of the pact. Everything except my feelings toward my Uncle Jack, for the reason that I was still confused about them.

He read carefully, commented upon the wording, satisfied himself that the pact was not fraudulent in purpose, complimented me upon my signature, and handed it back with his blessing.

"You have made a pact with dizzards," he said, looking at me steadfastly. "And may the devil fetch them should they turn against you. Which they will at the first chance."

"I have plans to protect myself."

"You must for they will not protect you."

We went back to the ship together. Tyndale spent the night, and together we loaded eight hundred Bibles at dawn.

"I'm working now on the Old Testament," Tyndale said. "Probably in Marburg near Frankfurt is where we'll print it. You can always reach me here, however, through James Curtis, my closest friend in Antwerp. He'll know me by the name Daltin henceforth, which you will note is like Tyndale with a couple of letters changed about."

"I'll use Daltin," I said. "It's good practice in these perilous times for men like you to change their names. I'll always ask for Daltin."

"Bye the bye," Tyndale said, "have you read the New Testament yet? Of course not. Why do I ask? Ask the birds. Ask the beasts."

"No, but I intend to. I will. I've been busy . . ."

"I wrote this book for you and for others like you," Tyndale said, trying hard not to sound like a schoolmaster.

We had already hidden the Bibles away in the secret place at the foot of the mainmast, but Tyndale extracted the wooden pins, let down the top timber, and, saying he wanted to give me one, took forth a fresh copy of his Testament. Now I had two.

Then he led me to my cabin and there wrote on the flyleaf *"Quod Amem,"* then below it in English, "Out of love," and signed his name.

"Which do you like?" he asked me. "Which strikes your ear and holds it most?"

"Out of love," I said.

I didn't see him again until the day I left for London. There was contraband corn to dispose of, which I did at a triple profit, a cargo to assemble, chiefly olive oil from Spain, and a mainmast to buy. The latter I shopped for everywhere and finally bought in Antwerp—a fine, straight timber grown in Sweden, somewhat shorter in length than commonly used by the English and German ships, but favored by the Spaniards since it was possible with a shorter mainmast to sail closer to the wind.

Even then, in April, I had begun to outfit for my first voyage to the Indies, which was Belsey's wish.

My last day in Antwerp I called on James Curtis, who dealt in groceries and had a warehouse with the English Adventurers, asking for Daltin instead of for Tyndale.

"He's leaving for Marburg," Curtis said. "Tomorrow, I think. And not too soon, as things are turning out. Ten days ago I had an unexpected caller. His name was Edward Lee, and he carried with him credentials from the King."

"Very high credentials?" I asked.

"This Edward Lee is ambassador to Spain and was on his way home," Curtis continued. "He said that the King was most anxious to get in touch with Tyndale and could I help. I told him that I knew no one by that name."

That evening Tyndale came down to the ship to give me a message.

"I'm leaving for Marburg, but I'll be back here soon again," he said. "I forgot to tell you that on Saturdays I spend the day with families who have been persecuted for their religion, driven from England, and have fled here for safety. They are poor and need help. If you learn to read the New Testament, you can go to the sail loft where they live and read it to them. There'll be days when I'll not be among the fishermen and days when I won't be with the persecuted. I don't wish to impose this upon you as a duty, but you may want to help when you're here."

"I don't promise to make the visits," I said. "But I do solemnly promise to read the Testament."

"If you read the Testament, you will make the visits," Tyndale said.

"Then I'll do both," I said.

"And keep a good watch also on your partner Belsey."

"May you go with God," I said.

And we embraced as we parted.

Chapter 29

By chance I saw King Henry just three days later when we returned to London.

We were waiting, our ship and his barge, to make the perilous trip between the arches of London Bridge, His Majesty on one side and we on the other. We were waiting for the tide to turn, so he could go downstream to Hampton Court and we to customs.

It had been a dreadful winter in London, cold mizzling days, the seas frozen, people eating flour made of beans, and, even through the winter months, fear of the plague. In Antwerp I had heard tales from captains traveling thither of nine or ten people dying each day. Now that it was early spring the number had increased.

It was a warm day with a breeze from far-off fields that smelled of newly cut hay. The breeze blew the royal banners straight out and made them snap like whips. I saw women in gay-colored dresses and courtiers with feathers in their hats.

Now and then I caught a glimpse of the King himself, pacing the deck with his long strides, his skin glowing pink beneath his white shirt, his broad shoulders—it was said they were three feet across—and his reddish hair giving him the look of a young athlete impatient to grapple with some monstrous foe. How grand he looked! How much the conquering king!

The tide ebbed, and the roar of the water rushing through the arches ceased. Now I could hear the sound of viols and lutes and other sweet instruments.

We passed two starlings away, but I caught a close glimpse of the king, still striding the length of the deck, shining with good health and spirits. If he was afraid of the plague that now gripped the city, there was no sign of his fear. The only way I knew that there was some concern on the royal barge was that I saw, as we passed within hailing distance, two pots aflame on the deck and caught the strong odor of burning ilex, whose fragrant smoke was thought to hold the plague at bay.

But they spoke of the plague at customs, and the first thing Belsey asked me was, "Did you see the King and his court fleeing down the river?"

"Is it that bad?" I said.

"More than three thousand dead of it last week. You didn't bring any with you?"

He was alarmed, so alarmed that it was a full minute before he thought to ask me how I had fared in Antwerp with the contraband corn and what kind of cargo I had brought in. Only when I informed him that we had tripled our money on the corn, that I had bought timber for a fine mainmast and olive oil at a price that assured us a handsome profit—only then did he manage a smile.

We went promptly to the goldsmith's and settled our account for the corn, and with my share I left at once for Clink, hoping to free my Uncle Jack; if not, then to improve his living conditions.

Samuel Carswell was present. I waited the better part of two hours to see him, yet he greeted me with one of his fleshy grins and bade me take a chair, where the sun was in my eyes and I had to squint to see him. He asked kindly about my voyage to Antwerp and about my profits therefrom. But he wasted no time getting down to the business at hand.

"As I informed you before," he said, "I cannot free your uncle until certain formalities are met. And formalities take time, especially now when so many of our officials have left the city. However, I can move Master Barton from where he now resides to more comfortable quarters. There he'll enjoy the morning sun, quiet, and the company of more inspiring companions."

"I'm a sailor," I reminded him, "with limited funds."

"A captain and a ship owner," Mr. Carswell corrected me. "For the advantages outlined I must have a stipend of five pounds, two pounds a week thereafter. And may I remind you," he said rising to his feet, "that we have a waiting list for the commodious quarters your uncle will occupy."

There was nothing to do except to pay the fee he demanded and do so as pleasantly as possible.

While I was closing the door on my way out, and as he stuffed the gold coin in his doublet, a thought struck him.

"Your uncle," he said, "has been feeling poorly the last few days, I am told. Mistress Nye has moved him to new quarters where he'll be more comfortable."

"Who is Mistress Nye?" I demanded.

"One of the helpers," Mr. Carswell said. "You might properly call her a nurse. Not a regular nurse, mind you. The regular nurses are all occupied with the sick. But a nurse she is, and you'll find her most accommodating."

"Where do I find Mistress Nye?"

He came around the desk, pressed past me, begging my pardon, and pointed down the corridor.

"There at the end is a turning. You take this turning to the left, then to the right. Here you'll come to a door, and beyond the door is a courtyard and across the courtyard is where you'll find Mistress Nye. That is, you'll find her in the vicinity."

On the way I paid another stipend to the old woman who kept the ledger and to the lean young man with the keys, who took me to the courtyard but would go no farther.

"That's where they keep the sick ones," he said, pointing, and quickly disappeared.

Mistress Nye met me at the door and led me up a short flight of stairs to a large, barren room with one window and thick straw on the floor.

There were a dozen bodies or more lying about, some quite still, others groaning and grinding their teeth. I stopped and stared at the scene before me, speechless and numb, it slowly dawning upon me that the place where I stood was the plague room. The pesthouse for Clink Prison.

Mistress Nye was a big woman, shaped like an Ionic pillar.

"Who is it you want?" she said. "We're busy here. Speak up. Maybe he's not here. We sent out a load of them last night."

"Captain Jack Barton," I said.

Mistress Nye knew everyone, no matter that they might have sunken cheeks and twisted mouths, that they crawled instead of walked, and even their loved ones didn't know them. She glanced around, knowing them all.

"Captain Barton? He didn't go out in the cart last night. No. They change fast. They come in looking fine, and in three hours they're dead. No, he's here. Over there in the corner. Yes, that's the captain and a brave one he is, too."

I knew Uncle Jack because of his beard and the fire in his eyes. Everything else was changed. He was shrunken and his chin drooped and he was the color of wet ashes. He could have been someone else.

He put out his hand but changed his mind and withdrew it. "I'm sick, boy, sick as a cur. But I'll be out. Did you bring money to pay my way?"

"We had a successful trip," I said. "As soon as you feel better, we'll have you on deck with all sails set."

He tried to turn over but failed. "Strong in the head but weak in the body," he grunted. "I must turn over, boy. I've got something here I need. Speaking of ships. Just the thing." I rolled him over, and he scrabbled around until he found a piece of paper, which he handed to me. "This is just in case, boy. I'm going to make it. When the wind blows, it's good to be ready with a reef, eh?"

It was a short sentence on a small piece of paper, written in a shaky hand, willing me in the event of his death all rights to the ship, the *Black Pearl*. He had had trouble signing his name, but it was there and under it the signature of Sarah Nye.

"Written, dated, witnessed, and delivered," he said. "All in proper order, eh?"

Trying to smile, I thanked him and put the paper away in my doublet. I could tell that he expected to be on his feet in a matter of days. Otherwise, he would never have made out the will and signed it. It's possible, however, that he was trying to avoid the jaws of hell, which vaguely loomed in his thoughts.

Nurse Nye said that she thought he would die before the night was out. Around three, she thought, since that was the hour most of them did die.

But Uncle Jack died at four o'clock instead of three, just as the death cart was passing, one man driving, another walking alongside, ringing his bell.

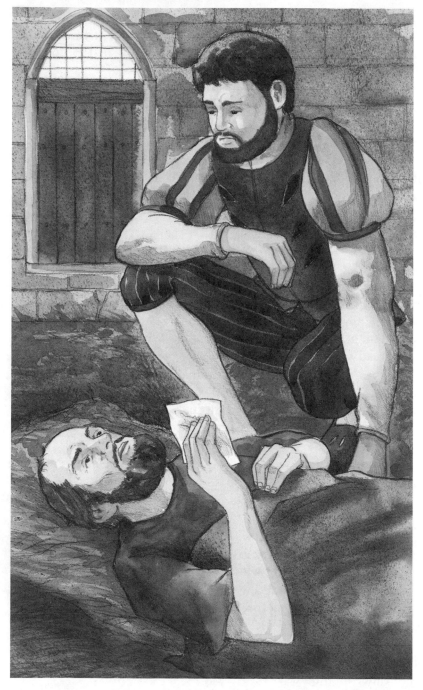

The nurse hailed the driver, and when she began to drag Uncle Jack across the floor, I rushed in to lift him up. But she pushed me away and called to the man with the bell.

"The plague is contagious," she said. "You catch it by touch. By a breath. By a look."

I argued with her. I said that I would take my uncle down the river and bury him far out at sea. She gave me another push, shoving me away from him.

"God bless us!" she cried. "You're daft."

The bell-ringer and cart driver took a part, and the two of them dragged Uncle Jack, still clutching a handful of straw, across the floor and down the stairs, his head bumping with a hollow sound on each of the three steps.

Together, they flung him into the death cart, already filled helter-skelter with piled-up bodies. The driver clucked to his horses, the bell-ringer rang his bell, and off they went along the dimly-lit street.

Chapter 30

Three weeks later, I came down with the sweating sickness myself, but fortunately for me not in the public pesthouse.

I had strength enough to drag myself through the town, down the embankment, and aboard the *Black Pearl*. A guard was posted at the dock and a red cross painted on the ship's hull, but at least I was safely at home.

I remember little of the plague except that I was always nauseated and that my head felt like a hard, green melon that at any moment would fly apart into a dozen pieces. I sweated away half my weight and all of my strength.

I thought I would die, at times wished that I would, but, although more than six thousand did die during that terrible summer, I managed to survive. Because, I believe, of the care of my faithful friend the ship's carpenter, Ed Groat, who, lovingly when he thought I was a goner, made me a proper coffin and lovingly carved an angel upon the oaken lid.

It took me until March of that winter to get my strength back and until May before I felt like venturing forth. It was a nightmarish time, but not all of it lost. For in those days I did two things of worth—I learned at last to read the English language—to read it well—and used my new skill during the days and the long hours of the night to read William Tyndale's translation of the New Testament, as I had promised him I would.

During this period of the plague I never heard from him, but I was sure in the knowledge that he had not yet been captured by the King, though the Lowlands and the provinces of Germany and France swarmed with royal and clerical spies.

I knew he was alive and free and busy at work because almost weekly Ed Groat brought me pamphlets, still fresh from the printery, that Tyndale had written against his violent enemies in England, those who in their violence called his work a "testament written by the devil himself."

All during my sickness I was in touch with Herbert Belsey, who sent me food and fond notes of encouragement. Later, when I was on the mend, he would ask me every few days how soon I would be able to take the *Black Pearl* to sea again. I never wrote back. Instead, I always sent word to him by Ed Groat, because Belsey feared that a letter from my hands might carry contamination.

I took the ship downriver to the Deptford boatworks in early summer, removed the cargo of Bibles, sent them by wherry in the middle of the night across the river, and sold them to a London dealer. The next morning we began to unstep the old mainmast and set the new one, a beautiful piece of timber, true as an arrow.

It was on the day after we had finished with the mast and were giving the hull a heavy coat of tar that my business with the New World Exploration and Trading Company really began.

The ship was careened, and I was standing with a tar brush in one hand and a bucket of hot tar sitting nearby when Belsey and Henry Phillips appeared on the bankside above me.

They looked out of place amidst all the muck and disorder, dressed as they were in velvet and silk. Ed Groat was working alongside me, and I could tell by the casual way he began to slap his brush around that nothing would please him more than to slop a little of the tar on the two gentlemen in their fine clothes.

Phillips shouted down, "What are you up to?"

It was obvious what we were up to, but since he was a valued shareholder I explained that we were coating the hull below the waterline with tar.

"What's that accomplish?" he asked.

From the tone of his voice I got the impression that he thought that we were down there just wasting time.

"The tar keeps worms out of the hull," I explained.

"Worms?" he said. "I thought worms burrowed around in the ground."

"Earthworms do," I said. "But sea worms burrow in wood. In two or three months' time they can chew a hull to pieces. They did it with Columbus' *Santa María.*"

"In two or three months, then, you'll have to tar the hull again."

"Scrape her down to the wood," I said, "give her a good sanding and then a thick coat of tar. Then you'll always have a shipshape hull. This hull is almost thirty years old, and she's as good as the day she was launched."

Phillips thought about this information for a moment or two. "I'd think you could coat the hull with something more permanent than tar. Save a lot of time and money, I'd think. Of course, I'm not a sailor."

Belsey said, "I hear that the Swedes are sheathing their ships with lead. It lasts for years."

"I've heard of this practice," I said. "But it's costly. Very costly here in England."

"Would you use lead if we could get our hands on some?" Phillips asked.

"Certainly, if it didn't cost more than tar." I didn't want the high price of lead to come out of my share of the profits. The ship had gotten along fine for years without lead sheathing.

"I can get lead cheap," Phillips said. "Loads of it. You'd have to melt it down, however."

"What do you think?" I asked Ed Groat, who knew a lot more about sheathing than I did.

"Melting's not the problem. It's the beating out that takes time."

"Would it be worth the trouble?" I asked.

"Depends on the lead," Groat said. "On the quality, let's say."

"The best quality," Phillips answered from the bank.

"There's quality, then there's quality," Ed Groat said. "Some's soft, too soft. Some's too hard. Where's this lead come from?"

A barge went by, and we waited until the waves subsided.

"Where from?" Ed asked again.

"From an abbey over near Wilton. The King's thinking of tearing it down, and I can buy up a lot of the lead cheap."

"Where's it coming from?" Ed asked. "From pipes, roofs, gutters, material like that?"

"From windows—stained-glass windows. Frames I think."

"That's the best kind," Ed Groat said. "That kind makes fine sheathing. Soft. Easy to melt down and roll out. Easy to handle all around."

I stopped painting and looked up at Phillips. "I wouldn't want to use lead taken from an abbey. From stained-glass windows," I said.

Phillips looked surprised. "Why?" he asked. "Lead's lead."

"It just doesn't seem rightful to use abbey lead this way."

"It's the King's command. You wouldn't be against the King's command, would you?"

"No, but I still don't think it's right to tear up stained window glass and melt down the lead for sheathing. Tar will do," I said, starting to paint again. "It has for a long time."

"I thought you'd be backing the King in his struggle to rid himself of that Spaniard, Carlos."

"I know he's threatened to take over the monasteries and all their lands," Ed Groat said.

"I honestly don't know much about the struggle," I said.

We had run out of tar, and I picked up the bucket and went over to the iron barrel that was heating over a fire.

Phillips strolled up to where I was stirring the bubbling tar, stepping carefully so as not to soil his boots. "It surprises me to find you against His Majesty."

"I'm not against His Majesty," I said.

Phillips watched me fill the bucket. Suddenly he said, "I always thought you were on the Church's side. But from what I've heard, you're against Sir Thomas More. I've heard too that you're a friend of Martin Luther's. And that other one. What's his name?" He glanced at Belsey for help.

"Tyndale," Belsey said. "William Tyndale."

"Yes, that's the name. Tyndale."

I went down the beach and began to paint again, working fast because the tide was coming in.

"By the way," Phillips said, stooping to wipe river mud from his boots. "You've seen his Bible, haven't you?"

"Yes, I've seen it," I said, deciding not to tell him that I had read it.

"Where did you see it?"

"In Antwerp. In London. In Deptford. Everywhere I've gone, nearly."

"It's very popular, all right," Phillips said. "Do you think we would profit by printing an edition in Antwerp and selling it here?"

"You'd have a right to print it in Antwerp. But it's against the law to bring it into England," I said.

I looked up at Phillips standing against the bankside, with the wind blowing his blond hair and the feather in his hat moving about, and I thought again, "I've seen this man before."

Phillips said, still cleaning his boots, "He's a law-abider, this young man."

"About Bibles," said Belsey, smiling his lopsided smile. "But about other things he's not so abiding."

"If we got a cargo of lead from the abbey," Phillips said, "not from the windows but from the roof and gutters, would you take it to Venice?"

"Lead stripped from an abbey, wherever it came from, I'd feel the same about," I answered.

The tide was catching the ship, moving it slowly upright, so I pulled out the longboat and Ed Groat and I got in with our bucket of tar and went on painting the bottom.

Belsey and Phillips climbed the bank out of the tide's reach and stood for a while watching us.

"When will you be finished with the tar?" Belsey asked.

"We'll careen again tomorrow," I said, "and paint the port side. We should be ready in three days. By Friday at the latest."

"Come down to the dock at Saint Catherine's Way when you're finished. We'll have a cargo ready for you. Not later than Friday evening."

They left the bank and walked off through the field toward their horses.

"What do you make of them?" Ed Groat asked me.

"They're after Tyndale," I said.

"What makes you so certain?"

"Everything Phillips said."

"Can he really get lead?"

"It's possible."

"How about the Bibles he wants to print and bring in?"

"There's already a new printing passing around. It comes from Antwerp, from a printer by the name of Endhoven. There'll be other printings. But Phillips isn't interested in bringing in Bibles. He's interested in getting his hands on Tyndale."

"And upon you, Tom, if you bring in a cargo of Bibles."

Belsey and Phillips had mounted their horses. As they rode past us, Phillips shouted, "We'll have a cargo of lead for you from Henry's palace."

He laughed and waved a gloved hand. It was his laughter that struck fire. It had some of the same harsh, rolling sounds that I had heard once before. Had I heard it on the night in Cologne when I had come from eating supper with Tyndale and had happened upon Belsey talking to a man at the street turning? As I had passed them, the man with Belsey had laughed at my horse.

Was it the same laughter that I heard now, fading away over the meadow, harsh, cruel, and derisive?

Chapter 31

We spent long hours getting the ship ready to sail.

By nightfall all I wanted to do was to eat and fall into my bunk, but for three nights I went around in Deptford trying to find out something about Henry Phillips.

Everyone knew Belsey, and everyone deduced from what they knew about him that a friend of his could not amount to much. But they would say no more, nor did they try to invent more, Deptford people being a close-mouthed group.

On Friday we took the ship to St. Catherine's dock, as promised, and there met my two partners. Phillips had been joking about the lead, of course, and the cargo of wool they were counting on had not arrived and did not arrive for three more days.

This gave me a chance to do more inquiring about Phillips. But, as at Deptford, my efforts failed, and I was on the point of giving up when it occurred to me that there was one man in London whom I had overlooked. A man with a large acquaintance in a city of gossip, rumor, and varieties of truth.

This thought came to me on Sunday night. Early the next morning I was in Mr. Carswell's office. I was there before he arrived, an hour before, waiting for him. He was flushed in the face and not too happy-looking when he came and kept me waiting for another hour before he called me into his office.

"I hope you're not bringing another one," he grumbled. "We're full to the garret. Have to put him up in the old pesthouse, which is not being used now. Not luxurious, but . . ."

"I'm here," I said, "to find out if you're acquainted with a man by the name of Phillips."

"Phillips? Who isn't acquainted with someone by the name of Phillips? A very common name in London, you know."

"Henry Phillips."

"That's different. Henry Phillips? That name has distinct possibilities."

Mr. Carswell called out to the old woman in charge of the brassbound ledger and asked her to bring it forth.

He spread the ledger out on his desk and thumbed through the pages until he came to the names beginning with the letter *P*. At this point he paused, read for several minutes, placed a ribbon marker on the page, closed the ledger, and looked up.

Mr. Carswell had not changed. He was a blunt man, and he was blunt now.

"Henry Phillips, Esquire, has been one of my respected guests here at Clink," he said. "Not once, but twice. There's a possibility that he might honor me with a third visit." He opened the ledger again and gave me an appraising look. "What's your connection with Mr. Phillips?"

There was nothing to be gained by being evasive with Samuel Carswell.

"He's a partner in a business we own called the New World Exploration and Trading Company," I said.

"He's a partner or he owns a share in the company? There's a difference, you know. Legally speaking."

"He's a shareholder."

"A large one?"

"He owns about a quarter of the shares."

"Has he paid for them?"

"Yes."

"In paper?"

"In gold."

Mr. Carswell made a questioning murmur in his throat. "Your company has an important-sounding name. Do your operations coincide with the name?"

"We're just starting. We have a cargo now ready for the Lowlands. We'll be trading regularly there and with Spain and Portugal. Likely with the Indies."

"What of the exploration that you mention?"

"We plan to explore, too, once we get started."

"In the New World?"

"There and in other places."

Mr. Carswell pondered. "Just how important is it for you to know the truth as I have it here?" He lifted the heavy ledger, held it up to my gaze, and set it down. "Are you just curious about Henry Phillips or are you in earnest? In other words, are you interested in knowing about him financially? His morals? His religion?"

"Everything you can tell me about him is important."

"How important?" Mr. Carswell asked without a pause. "Enough to settle a share of your company upon me?"

"I have gold."

"A share," repeated Mr. Carswell. "I wouldn't refuse a little gold, either. But trading and exploration is a growing business. A ship, as you know, has already gone around the world. Where ships go, trade follows. I would rather share the future with you than the present. A share in your next venture, is it?"

"A share."

"How many?"

"Five."

"Say seven and I'll give you all the information on Henry Phillips you'll ever have use for."

At that moment I would have given everything I owned to know what was written in the brassbound ledger that lay in front of me.

Mr. Carswell excused himself and repaired to an alcove where I heard the gurgle of something flowing from a jug. He came back briskly, opened the ledger, and began to talk rather than read from the notes he had taken upon the occasions Henry Phillips had been in Clink.

"First off," said Mr. Carswell, "as you'd perhaps guess, Henry Phillips is well born. He's the son of Richard Phillips, a man of note in the counties of Dorset and Somerset, who was thrice a member of Parliament and twice high sheriff. He owns besides rich lands in many places."

"How ever did his son get in Clink?" I asked. "Which if my memory serves me right is reserved for the middling poor."

"There are ways and ways to matriculate," said Mr. Carswell. "And Henry chose one of many. Whether he was intended for the ministry is not clear. But he did have high ecclesiastical patrons, for two of them came here to persuade me to release him. However, he seemed to favor a literary career and spoke of it often to me."

Here Mr. Carswell retired again to the alcove and returned shortly, a little redder in the face, to resume his narrative.

"There are two convergent stories at this point," he said, "and I cannot vouch for either. But let me elucidate further and you can be the judge. One story is that in dire financial straits he deliberately robbed his father of a large sum of money and fell at once into disgrace. This is the story told and repeated and sworn to by his enemies. There is another story, however, a kinder version told by his friends, which I am at times inclined to believe. From this story, it appears that his father entrusted him with a large sum of money to pay some person or other here in London. But upon reaching the city, the son allowed himself to be tempted into a card game and in a single night gambled away the whole amount his father had placed in his care."

"Both stories could be true," I said.

"Yes, he could have stolen the money from his father and gambled it away."

"You spoke of Henry Phillips' joining the ministry of the Church," I said. "He's not a Lutheran, then?"

"God bless us, no!" exclaimed Mr. Carswell.

"I presumed not. For he speaks ill of Martin Luther and of Tyndale too."

"Equally. He's against heretics. He's against Lutheranism. If he had the power, he'd see that both Tyndale and Luther were hanged from the highest tree on Tower Hill."

"I gathered this from what he's said to me."

"Curiously enough," Mr. Carswell said, "he's strong too against the King. I advised him while he was my guest here at Clink to restrain himself or one day he'd find himself walking around without a head."

"He had money when he signed the contract with me. A bagful of it. That might account for his arrogance."

"His finances ebb and flow like the tide. It would be wise for him to take a more middle course."

Carswell had gone through his ledger and I think the jug of spirits as well. In any event, he said he would have a proper contract drawn up and that we would gather and sign it on the morrow, God willing.

"I wish Henry Phillips were not a partner in our next venture," he said as we parted. "But maybe we can change his ways. He's not a bad sort. Just a man of extremes."

I picked up my hat and made a stiff bow. I said nothing more, having already made up my mind about Henry Phillips.

Chapter 32

We had decided to take a cargo of wool to Antwerp, but a day before our sailing, on the advice of Belsey and Henry Phillips, the plans were suddenly changed.

The night before we were to sail, Belsey climbed over the bulwarks and strode across the deck to where Ed Groat and I were making an adjustment on the steering gear. The gear was sound but had a movement that I didn't like when the ship was in a following sea.

"I observe that you're all battened down," Belsey said cheerily, though he looked as if he needed a week's sleep. "All ready for heavy weather."

"Weather's good in the Channel," I said. "A ship in this morning from Antwerp reported fine sailing."

"Well," said Belsey, "Phillips and I were reading Fugger's newsletter last night at the Anchor and Chain and learned that wool's down ten percent in Antwerp and up seven in Venice. So we decided, knowing that you'd agree with us and want the best deal possible, to pass Antwerp and send the cargo to Venice."

By contract I held a controlling interest in the New World Company. I could have said that the ship was scheduled for Antwerp, that I was sailing for Antwerp, and that we would store the wool until the price improved.

Instead, I went on with my work in silence, while Belsey paced back and forth, waiting for my word.

If we changed our sailing from Antwerp to Venice, it meant that I would not be able to talk to Curtis, Tyndale's friend, or, unless I was fortunate, even get a message to Tyndale. And a message was important. It was a matter, I firmly believed, of life and death.

The meeting on the beach with Phillips, when Groat and I were tarring the hull, had convinced me that Belsey and Phillips were in league against Tyndale.

I was certain now that they had been together in Cologne, that actually I had seen Phillips there, that the talk about sheathing the ship with lead taken from the Wilton Abbey was only a ruse, an effort to find out how I felt about the King's confiscation of Church property.

The information I had drawn from Carswell confirmed what I already suspected about Phillips. Although there were many opposed to William Tyndale, none of them exceeded Phillips in hatred.

There were many, I truly believe, at that moment in the Low Countries, in Germany, and in France—upward of a hundred spies and agents—all of them on the trail of the translator of the New Testament, but none more violently against him than Phillips.

There was one, for instance, Francis Birkman, a bookbinder in Antwerp, who even tried to buy up a whole pipe of these Bibles from a shop in Frankfurt in order to burn them.

And John Hackett, English ambassador in the Low Countries, was instructed by Chancellor Wolsey, the King's closest advisor, to discover the printer of Tyndale's books, to gather them together, and send them to London for burning. Instead, all the copies that could be found were seized and burned in Bergen-op-Zoom.

Belsey came over to where I was working with Ed Groat. "What decision have you come to?" he asked. "We've already made up our minds. Venice is our best opportunity."

"I haven't come to any decision," I said. "I'll let you know what I think when I'm through with the tiller. We can't go anywhere until it's fixed."

The tiller was already fixed, but I went on puttering around, thinking hard, and decided at last that I would go to Antwerp first, talk to Tyndale if he was there, leave a message if he was not, then sail on to Venice. A two- or three-day stopover in Antwerp was of no importance in a voyage of this length.

But the decision came suddenly to naught, as Henry Phillips climbed aboard and announced that he would like to go as far as Seville with us.

"We'll sail with the tide," I said, "and the tide will ebb at four." The bells at St. Paul's had just struck the hour of one. "That gives you three hours to get yourself aboard."

I excused myself with a captain's curt bow and went at once to my cabin. There I wrote a long letter to Tyndale relating all that I had learned in my talks with Phillips, the information about his character I had gained from Warden Carswell, and my own beliefs about his violent intentions.

I sealed the letter carefully, went out immediately on the waterfront, and searched diligently until I found a captain whom I trusted and who was making the voyage to Antwerp within the week.

Carswell had confirmed something more than my suspicion that Phillips desired to destroy Tyndale's work. He had proved, to me at least, that Phillips desired to destroy Tyndale himself. Furthermore, I was certain that Phillips was well supplied with gold—money that he had received from rich men in London who were equally determined upon Tyndale's destruction.

Many said that it was a ruthless man named John Stokesley who furnished the gold to Phillips, because he had often bragged that he had killed more heretics than any one else alive.

Chapter 33

Phillips was late coming aboard, but we still made the tide and arrived off Gravesend in time to catch a strong prevailing wind, under a fair sky, and make a good heading across the Bay of Biscay.

We had fine sailing until, off the southern coast of Portugal, we encountered heavy seas. Everyone in the crew had a touch of seasickness, but Phillips came down with it hard. I must say, however, that he bore it with a fortitude I didn't expect from him.

Our plans to sail directly to Seville were thwarted at the mouth of the Guadalquivir, where heavy rains had blocked the entrance with shifting silt. After a day of struggling to get the heavy-laden ship through the entrance, we gave up and sailed to Cádiz farther to the south. Phillips set off from Cádiz on horseback for Seville, and we took a straight course for the Ionian Sea.

We had picked up a knowledgeable pilot in Cádiz and made Venice as smoothly as if we were sailing on an English lake.

Our wool brought a good price, and we bought Venetian glass and silk with the profits, sailing south again after a short week in this most beautiful of cities, feeling quite proud of ourselves, both as merchants and seamen.

The Guadalquivir was open when we arrived, and we negotiated the winding river without mishap, though with the help of a Spanish seaman whom we hired from one of the ships lying at anchor in the river entrance.

Our Spaniard's name was Juan de Palos. He had, so he said, been born in Palos and sailed from there with Columbus and had been imprisoned with him as well.

I deeply appreciated Juan de Palos. He looked like a Spanish brigand, or like my idea of a brigand, with wild eyes and one cropped ear and a gold ring in the other, but he was a good and grizzled pilot.

We had not been in Seville an hour before he was proposing that we outfit the *Black Pearl* for a voyage to the New World.

I had dreamed many times of sailing off to the Indies. The tales of gold and green continents and pink coral beaches and great cities in the jungle where no one lived, islands where there were no men, only fair-haired women taller than a tall man— all these I dreamed of on idle watches at sea.

"But, señor, there is one condition," Juan said in his soft Sevillian accent. "I am the pilot. The license must be written in my name. You are English, see, and therefore cannot become a pilot in a country that belongs to Spain."

I hired him on the spot, gave him some gold and a shove toward the entrance of La Casa de Contratación, which was next door to the Alcazar. It was there I was to meet Henry Phillips. "Go," I said, "and become a pilot licensed to sail in the waters of the New World. We'll sail together, maybe."

He did so, and joined us the next day.

Then, as planned, I met Phillips in the Alcazar, not that day but the next, less than two months from the afternoon when we had parted at Cádiz.

He had grown a sweeping Spanish mustache with waxed, turned-up tips, and wore a short sword in a Cordovan sheath at his side. What he had done meanwhile he did not say, nor did he have anything in the way of merchandise to show.

Truth was, Henry Phillips didn't consider himself a merchant. It was an occupation beneath his dignity as a gentleman. To buy and sell goods, to go into the fields and warehouses and haggle over prices, was something he would disdain.

But I was certain that he had not been idle since I had seen him last. Charles V, Emperor of the Holy Roman Empire, the most powerful ruler on earth, was now in Seville.

It was most likely that Phillips had come to Seville for the one purpose of seeking an audience with him. The Emperor had heard of Tyndale, despised him, and could play an important part in any plot against him. What was more logical, therefore, than that the two should meet to discuss the English heretic!

We left Seville with half a cargo, fortunately none of it subject to spoilage, for off Portugal our balky tiller jumped its gudgeons and we had to put in at Lisbon for repairs, which took eight days.

Then, upon entering the Bay of Biscay, Phillips came down with a mysterious sickness, which he had apparently contracted in Lisbon.

It was my advice that we head straight for England, but he was unswerving in his demand that we stop at Antwerp where, he said, he would receive better treatment than in London. Against my judgment I humored him in this and, though we could have made faster time by sailing a more westerly course, I piled on all canvas and made for Antwerp.

After a day on this new course, he seemed to worsen and in the evening asked Groat if we had a Bible on the ship. Groat asked me, and I pondered the wisdom of letting Phillips have one of my two copies of Tyndale's New Testament, the only version of the Bible we had on board.

At last, with misgivings, I took to his cabin the one that did not have Tyndale's inscription to me. He was too sick, or claimed to be, to read, so I read to him several passages out of Matthew. One passage he asked me to read twice:

> *Come unto me all ye that labor and are heavy laden, and I will ease you. Take my yoke on you and learn of me, for I am meek and lowly in heart: and ye shall find rest unto your souls. For my yoke is easy, and my burden is light.*

He didn't respond to the readings, lying with his face half-covered, uttering no sound or comment. And soon I realized that I was reading to a man who had fallen asleep. I left the Bible on the table beside his bed in case he wished to read when he woke up.

Ed Groat greeted me outside the cabin. "I think Phillips is done for. Not the plague, thanks to the Lord, but something bad."

I agreed that Phillips' chances looked poor. "Get out the coffin you made for me. We'll give him a decent burial, though I don't know exactly why we should," I said.

"Neither do I," said Groat. "But I'll make a new lid. I'll keep the one with the angel that I carved for you. A plain lid is more suitable somehow."

The next day Phillips was improved, so much so that I again suggested we alter course and head for London, but he still insisted upon sailing to Antwerp.

He was quite well when we reached there, and disappeared as soon as the ship docked.

I watched him swing jauntily along the dock toward town. I had the awful conviction that at last he was on Tyndale's trail, at last armed with papers and writs and all the paraphernalia he would need.

He was on his way to find and arrest Tyndale in the name of Charles V.

That night when I went to get Tyndale's Bible from the shelf above my bunk, I discovered that it was missing. I remembered then that I had not put it back when I had finished reading it to Phillips. I searched the cabin. The disturbing thought struck me that Phillips had taken it along with him when he left the ship that afternoon.

Chapter 34

James Curtis, I was disappointed to learn, had not received the letter I had written to Tyndale. An odd happening, since couriers between the two cities were usually prompt even in time of war.

Equally disappointing was the fact that Curtis had no idea where Tyndale was.

Numerous pamphlets had come down the Rhine with Tyndale's name on them, apparently sent from somewhere in the vicinity of Frankfurt, but there had been no direct word between them. Indeed, no word had come from Tyndale to anyone at the English Adventurers'.

I had always had trouble understanding the language spoken by Tyndale's friends on Fishtail Row, so I went to the abandoned sail loft where the English dissenters lived. It was a cold day and twenty of them—men and women and children—were huddled around a fire they had built up from dried kelp. There was a pot filled with fish heads and gobbets of something black stewing over the fire.

Sarah Williams, a stout woman in man's boots, with black hair cinched tight on her skull, was the leader of the group. I asked her if she had seen Tyndale since the last time we had been there together.

"No," she said. "We've had only one message from him in weeks."

"A month and longer," some man put in.

"It came from Marburg," Mistress Williams said. "He was at the university there. Studying, I guess. Writing, too."

"It appears then that he's free," I said.

"Free, yes. If you want to call hiding in cellars and fields free. And going around disguised, too, so even his friends don't know him or speak to him. Like a spirit. Like a dead man."

I told Sarah Williams about the message that I had sent to Tyndale in the care of James Curtis and everything that I had put in it.

"The message didn't get here?" she asked.

"It didn't get to Curtis, I know."

"What do you think if I went to Marburg and gave Tyndale the message you told me about?" Sarah Williams said.

"I think it's a good idea. Perhaps not for you to go, but someone in the group who's not so well known. Tell Tyndale everything I have just told you. Also that Phillips has been to Seville to talk to Charles the Fifth and that he came here to Antwerp yesterday with me."

It was agreed that one of the men would leave that night for Marburg. I shared some of the awful fish-head soup with them and went back at once to give James Curtis the news from Sarah Williams.

I was leaving at a late hour when Henry Phillips came in with some young friends. He greeted me civilly and said that he was sorry that he wouldn't be able to go back to England with the ship.

"Would it be possible," he said, drawing aside from his friends, "for you to give me an advance on the cargo you sold in Venice?"

I had the money, and I could have handed it over to him without any inconvenience to myself, but I refused him.

"I'll settle with you in London," I said. "At the same time I settle with Belsey and Carswell." I turned away and stopped. "You have my Tyndale Bible," I reminded him. "We sail around noon tomorrow. Without fail, leave it here before you go. Without fail, understand?"

He paused and clenched his brow as if about to say something of importance, then changed his mind and said, "I'll see you in London inside the week."

I didn't expect to see him in London. In fact, I was never to see him in London, although I was to see him soon again.

We sailed at noon the next day without, of course, Tyndale's Bible, which Phillips had failed to deliver. Wind and tide were favorable, and we made a quiet passage to London.

It was made quieter by Juan de Palos, who entertained me with tales of the New World he had visited with the great Columbus. Some were fantastical; some sounded true. But true or false, they fired my imagination.

Juan de Palos had a full store of suggestions. For one thing, he called the New World *"El Otro Mundo,"* the Other World, and wished me to do so.

"You must also change the name of the ship," he said. "All ships that go to the Other World must have an official name. The name should be the name of a saint, like the *Santa María.* She must also have a nickname. We called her *'Las Gallegas,'* the Galician."

"What else, Juan?" I asked, now well into the spirit of the adventure.

"You must also carry an hourglass. Only it's a half-hour glass and we carried one on the *Niña.* The sand would run out every half-hour exactly and then we would turn it upside down, make a mark, and start over. Eight turnovers made a watch, you see."

"Who'll do the turning every half-hour?"

"I will," said Juan. "I am a great turner, and we never lacked for good time when I did the turning."

"What else?"

"We shall have square sails."

Furthermore, Juan had dreams of entering London at the head of a cavalcade amid music of trumpets and harps and the firing of cannon.

"We'll have cages of bright-colored parrots, and a chieftain with a golden collar and a basket full of pearls as big as pigeon eggs. And the chieftain will have a crown, like those I have seen in the Other World, very big and tall, with wings on its sides and golden eyes as large as silver cups."

"All we'll lack," I said, still fascinated with Juan and his Other World, "is Columbus himself."

"You will be the Columbus."

"But I lack his red hair and blue eyes."

"Those in your city, they do not know about the hair and the eyes," said Juan de Palos.

"But I am much younger than Columbus."

"You can be his son Diego," said my resourceful friend. "But better yet, you can be a new Columbus. And your ship, the *Black Pearl,* which looks much like Columbus' little *Niña,* can be a new *Niña,* We can paint her hull with the colors of your country and have big banners flying from all the masts."

"It sounds beautiful," I said, as we sped on our way with following seas and fair weather.

Chapter 35

We made a quick turnaround in London. The first morning we sold all of our Venetian glass at a handsome profit to the Duke of Wolten, and by noon had disposed of our casks of Spanish oil.

Straight off I went to see Master Carswell at Clink Prison, paying him more than one hundred percent for his profit in the venture. He was speechless with surprise, since he had expected not more than a third of that amount, and immediately wanted to reinvest half his gains in our next voyage.

"I don't know what our next voyage will be," I told him. "I'd advise you, therefore, to hold your gains until we have something with definite prospects. Perhaps four or five weeks from now."

We talked for an hour, or at least he did, and when he had unwound, I asked him if he had heard anything about Henry Phillips.

"As you know, he went as far as Seville with us," I said. "Then we picked him up and left him in Antwerp. That was three days ago. The Emperor was in Seville, and I think that Phillips had an audience with him."

"I can assure you that he did," Carswell said, counting for the second time the gold ducats I had given him, laying them out one by one on the table, then stacking them in one pile, and then starting the process over again. "They met three times in as many days, and their talk was mostly about Tyndale. The Emperor is determined to catch him."

"And Henry Phillips is the agent chosen to do so?"

"There are dozens of agents, as you know. But Phillips has met Tyndale sometime in the past. Perhaps when they were at Oxford. Anyway, Tyndale knows Phillips and for some reason likes him."

"What of Belsey?" I asked. "Is he mixed up in it in any way? He has been, but is he now?"

"Only as a servant, a go-between for Phillips. It was Phillips who got Belsey his job as searcher. They work together in all things. But Belsey is here and Phillips is across the Channel."

I left Carswell counting his Spanish ducats and went to the ship. The hold was half-filled with wool, and there was more to come the next day, according to Belsey, who was supervising the work.

Belsey and I had talked several times since I had arrived the previous evening, but not once had he mentioned the name of Henry Phillips. It struck me as odd, so odd that I concluded that Belsey knew where Phillips was and what he was doing. There was no need for him to ask.

I was convinced of this when Belsey informed me that the ship was cleared for Hamburg and would be ready to sail the following night, provided the wool arrived as promised.

"I was planning on Antwerp," I said. "I have two orders there, both of them subject to spoilage and both with merchants who depend upon me."

Belsey's face flushed. Only the scar around his mouth showed white. "You can go to Antwerp after Hamburg," he said. "The Hamburg order is equally important."

He spoke in a tone that he had not used with me since the day he had threatened to seize the ship unless I agreed to the contract he had prepared. It was a chilling memory.

Our talk took place at mess time. Shortly afterward, Belsey left the ship. He was gone past the hour of eleven, when the tide began to set. When it did set, with the ship half-loaded and the hatches open, we slipped our mooring. With Ed Groat and Juan de Palos and two men as crew, I headed downstream on the swift-running current under a hopeful new moon.

I sailed straight to Antwerp, but arrived there two days late because of a severe thunderstorm. I went to see James Curtis at once, though it was past midnight, and routed him out of bed. He had not seen Phillips, he told me as he stood shivering in his nightshirt and stocking cap, nor heard from William Tyndale.

The hour was advanced, but I went to the loft where the English dissenters lived. Stumbling over bodies in the dark where only a small cresset burned, I finally located Sarah Williams.

She must have been waiting for me, for she was fully clothed and instantly jumped to her feet.

It was a bitter night. We stood by the smoldering cresset, both of us too cold to talk easily, doing little more than mumble our words.

"Tyndale is here," she said, "here in Antwerp. He's living at the house of Thomas Poyntz, an English friend. He's been here now for almost two months. He rarely goes out, I am told; then only for a short while and usually at night."

"Where does Poyntz live?" I asked her.

"Near the Adventurers."

"Have you seen Phillips?" I said. "Or heard of him?"

"Neither one nor the other."

We parted, and I had to wait until the next afternoon to locate Poyntz. He lived in a large house on a quiet street, which he kept for members of the English Merchant Adventurers Company. At first he denied that he knew Tyndale.

"I've heard the name, is all," he said.

"You know who he is, however."

"Yes."

"You know that he is being sought."

"By whom?"

"The Emperor, the King, and by a hundred agents. Aren't you fearful of your own life if he's found living here in your house?"

This remark helped some, and piece by piece I assured him that I was Tyndale's friend. "I carried his first Bible into London," I said. "The first."

"Your name," he said at last, "is Tom Barton, and Tyndale has spoken of you."

"You are in danger. I am in danger. And Tyndale is in danger. Tyndale above all," I said.

"What's to be done at this hour?"

"Tyndale must flee. To Hamburg or Wittenberg or Worms or Mainz. Anywhere. There's no protection for him here. Margaret of Austria is the Emperor's regent. She is the law in the Low Countries. What he wants done, she must do. And he wants Tyndale captured."

"Tyndale's weary of flight. He has fled now for years. From cockcall to garret. From barn to cellar, from town to city to village, never knowing one hour of peace or sense of safety."

"The fleeing has been for nothing if he stays here in Antwerp. How long has he been with you?"

Thomas Poyntz was a well-fleshed man with an eater's round stomach. "For almost two months. But very quietly," Poyntz said. "He never goes on the street during the day. He does not parade himself."

"If the procurator-general and his sheriffs were to come today," I said, "with a writ from the Regent Margaret and search out your house, would they find evidence of him—his clothes, his books, his letters?"

"Yes, he's not that well hidden."

"Then, in God's name, he must leave the house."

"He's been here now for two months and in safety."

"But not with Henry Phillips in the city."

"Phillips has been in Antwerp several times in the last year. He is, in fact, a friend of Tyndale's. They have a common interest in the Bible. They talk together. They sometimes eat together. They go sometimes at night together to walk in the streets."

I could not believe what I had heard. Tyndale and Phillips friends? I described Phillips to Poyntz, his fair countenance, his manner of speaking, his way of dressing. I could not believe we were talking about the same man.

"You describe the Henry Phillips I have met," Poyntz said. "And know well."

"And this man is a friend of William Tyndale's?"

"A friend," Poyntz said, seemingly annoyed that I had raised the question. "A close friend."

Chapter 36

At that moment, unknown to me, Tyndale was at work in the house while Poyntz and I stood there talking.

It was near nightfall, and I was about to leave when he came into the room and threw his arms around my shoulders. His body felt like the body of a child, like someone who has starved for many weeks; he seemed more wraith than a man.

I greeted him in French, and we both laughed at my bad accent. He seemed in a happy mood as he complimented me on my luxuriant sideburns and wondered if I would ever stop growing.

"Have you seen my third revision of the New Testament?" he asked abruptly. "They say it's better than the first two. You wouldn't have had a chance to read it."

"No, I've been away," I said. "In Venice."

"You wouldn't find it there, would you?"

"Not likely."

"Henry Phillips tells me that he went with you as far as Seville and came back with you. And that you gave him much comfort when he was ill reading to him from the Testament. He speaks very highly of you, Tom. I am glad that you have become friends, for he is a fine young man."

I was shocked beyond the ability to speak or move. I stood there staring at Tyndale.

My hat, which I had dropped when he came into the room and which I had forgotten, was lying at my feet and Poyntz's little terrier was about to lift his leg upon it. Poyntz reached out with his foot and nudged the dog away, in the very nick of time, with no damage done except to the dog's pride.

Tyndale chortled and said, "*Si sic omnia,*" which I think but am not certain means, "If only everything had been like this."

Mrs. Poyntz appeared suddenly and left, taking the dog with her. Then Mr. Poyntz, who wore a riding cloak, asked to be excused since he was on his way to a town near Brussels and was already late. Tyndale and I were left alone, standing in the middle of the room, Tyndale smiling and I still too shocked to move or speak.

At last I got myself together and asked him if he had received a letter, a long letter, written by me some weeks before.

"It was not delivered to me. I wondered then why I didn't hear from you. Is there news that I should know now?"

I remembered the letter well. I could have repeated it to him word for word.

But I was struck with sudden doubts. Did I know for certain that Phillips had stolen money from his father and gambled it away? Did I really know that he had gone to talk to the Emperor against Tyndale and to plan his ruin? Might not it have been the opposite, that instead he had spoken to the Emperor on Tyndale's behalf? Could he not be, as Tyndale so strongly felt, his closest, most loyal friend?

While we stood again in silence looking at each other, Tyndale waiting for a reply, my thoughts totally confused, Henry Phillips came into the room. He greeted Tyndale with a Spanish *embrazo* and me with a smile, seemingly not in the least surprised to find me there.

"I am on my way to supper," he said. "Would you like to join me?" His invitation I felt was meant for Tyndale, but he did turn in my direction as if to include me. "I know a likely place for food and it would please me if you—if both of you—were to come along."

Tyndale said to Phillips, "Mistress Poyntz is roasting two ducks and wants you to stay for dinner. She'll be greatly disappointed if you don't." Then he turned to me, "And you too, my son. She will be put out if you don't stay to sample her wares."

"Thank her for the kindness," Phillips said. "I would do so myself, but I have pressing business after dinner and must be on my way. Come, the two of you."

Tyndale wondered if he needed a cloak, but Phillips, assuring him that the evening was mild, gently urged him toward the door. At the door Tyndale courteously stepped aside to allow Phillips and me to go first, but Phillips bowed and urged him on. I fell in behind them.

The door led into a narrow corridor, long, and at this time of day, since candles had not yet been lighted, quite dark. Phillips was tall, and I couldn't see the small figure of Tyndale moving along as we all walked slowly toward the street. I could hear him laughing, however, about something that Phillips had said.

Outside there was still a little light. The tops of the trees were quite golden with the sun's last glow, and a few lamps were coming on in the distance.

Of a sudden Tyndale must have stopped, for Phillips stopped too. The laughing ceased. And it seemed for a moment as if Tyndale had turned around. Perhaps, I thought, to go back for his cloak, because a cool wind was now coming through the entrance and down the corridor.

Then over Phillips' shoulder, against the fading light, I saw two figures standing at the entrance of the house, one on each side of the door.

At the same moment I saw Phillips make a sign, two quick thrusts of his hand, pointing down and in front of him, toward Tyndale.

Tyndale did not pause again or turn back, though he could plainly see what lay before him. It was almost as if he had expected this betrayal, that someday it might come, and that it was God's will that it should come now.

He walked down the dark corridor and to the entrance of Poyntz's home. He walked quickly, as if there were a hurry, into the waiting hands of the two sergeants-at-arms, who, posted there by a writ from the procurator-general, had been alerted by Phillips' sign.

In the golden light his face was serene. He said nothing and showed no surprise, even when the sergeants tied his hands behind him and walked him away in the darkness that had now fallen upon us.

In horror I looked around for Henry Phillips. I looked everywhere, my sword in hand, ready to use. The street was deserted. He had gone. He had disappeared among the trees as if he had never been.

BOOK FIVE

Chapter 37

A crowd began to gather as Tyndale was marched down the street.

Windows opened and people put their heads out cautiously, but no one spoke. It was very quiet, except for the noise of feet on the cobbles and the opening and closing of windows. Antwerp was a city under the thick thumb of Margaret of Hungary, the Queen Regent, aunt of the Emperor, Charles V.

I knew where the sergeants-at-arms lived. It was in a small, fortresslike house, with several other sergeants, quite near the headquarters of the English Adventurers. It had once been used as a jail, but it was now run-down, a lopsided building with thin slits for windows and a barred wooden door.

I went at once to Fishtail Row. I went from house to house. Everyone was at supper. Fishing had been good for the past week, and every table in every house was filled with food. I had no special friends among the fishermen, but Tyndale knew them all by their first names, had given them food and money when he had it to give.

John Schott was the first fisherman I stopped to see.

He was a leader among the group and especially liked by Tyndale. Schott was sitting in front of an immense bowl of fish stew, a large wooden spoon in one hand and a chunk of bread in the other.

He politely asked me to sit down and shoved a chair in my direction. He had five children and a wife, and they all had big bowls of stew in front of them. Perspiring from the hot soup, happy and flushed, no one stopped eating or looked up.

I thanked Schott for his kindness but did not sit down. In a few words I told him of Tyndale's plight.

"He's in jail now," I said. "The old one near the English Adventurers. It's lightly guarded and can easily be forced. A dozen of us can overcome it. My ship is at dock, and we can have him out of the harbor, out of the country, before dawn."

Everyone began to eat more slowly. Schott stopped eating first. He looked at me as if I were a sergeant who had come to make an arrest.

"I have a family," he said, making a gesture to take everyone into the fold. "I can't risk my life in such a scheme. Ask Worde. He lives next door. He is without a family and responsibilities."

He picked up his spoon and began to eat.

Leaving the Schotts', I went next door to see Worde, who was at a long bench with three other men. They were eating fish they had caught that day and were throwing the heads on the floor for three gray cats.

They were all husky young men and, like Schott, friends of Tyndale. They all gave me the same excuse. The moon was right, and they were leaving within an hour for the fishing grounds. Fish were running, for the first time in weeks. They dared not lose a chance to cast their nets.

"We have to fish or starve," Worde said. "Come in a week, and we'll go with you. We'll take the place apart stone by stone and throw the stones in their faces."

Everyone agreed that in a week they would be ready and anxious to help free their friend Tyndale.

"We can't wait a week. We can't wait even a day," I said. "It must happen now."

The four men shrugged and were silent, not moving, looking hungrily at the uneaten fish on their plates.

I went back to the ship to gather the crew, but Groat and two of the men had gone into the city, leaving Juan de Palos on watch. I told him what had taken place, but it was not very clear to him because he spoke little English.

He went to his cabin and came back with a dagger strapped to his thigh. We decided not to look for Groat and the rest of the crew, who we knew from experience would be scattered over the city. Instead we went to the loft of Sarah Williams.

The group was gathered and was likewise at supper, ladling from a bowl simmering over a cresset.

"Tyndale's been arrested," I said, even before I closed the door behind me.

"By whose order?" Sarah Williams shouted.

"By the Queen's."

"Bad," someone said.

"Where's he held?" Sarah asked.

"At the old jail."

She dropped her spoon in the pot, disappeared for a moment, and came back with a harvesting scythe in her hand. Others got up and left and came back with weapons of various kinds. Even a young woman with a child carried out a heavy-handled fisherman's hook.

There were eleven of us altogether as we came close upon the jail, one being Ed Groat, whom we picked up on the way. We gathered under a tree, in the dark, within sight of the one lantern burning at the door of the jail.

"This is what we'll do. Listen carefully," I said. "You are to stay here and say nothing and do not move about. I'll go on to the jail. I'll tell the sergeant that I have come with Tyndale's coat, which will be the one I am presently wearing. There will be at least six men guarding the jail. I happen to know this— I know it because upon two occasions I have had to bail out Juan de Palos for being pugnacious. There'll be six of them; I'll give the head sergeant seven gold sovereigns to share among his friends. If luck is with us, he'll take me to the cell. I'll hand over my coat, and tell Tyndale our plans in a few words.

"It shouldn't take more than three minutes to do this, once I am inside the jail. Keep track of the time, Juan de Palos, you being a good keeper of time. And when the door opens to let me out and light shines on the street, walk in. All of you, without words or cries or undue noise."

"The gold sovereigns will do the trick," Juan de Palos said.

"They are important," I said. I took them out of my doublet and gave them a good polishing on my sleeve. "Of the utmost."

At my knock an older sergeant, with more braid on his shoulders than those who had seized Tyndale, opened the massive door. I quietly slipped inside and held out the cloak at the same time that I showed him the gold sovereigns.

We were alone. At least I saw no one else in the room, which was poorly furnished and had two old dogs lying beside a fire flickering under an iron kettle.

The sergeant took me a short way to a door that had a lock but was not locked, and handed over the cloak to Tyndale, who as he looked at me seemed much calmer than I was.

"Your friends are outside," I told him casually in English. "Ed Groat, Juan de Palos, and eight of the dissenters, all armed. You are to follow us, the guard and me, when we leave, and slip into the street when the door is opened. The ship is at the dock, ready . . ."

The sergeant was looking at the gold sovereigns to make certain that they were what they were supposed to be.

"Someone will be killed," Tyndale said.

"Perhaps the sergeant," I replied.

"Others. The dissenters," Tyndale said. "The sergeant also."

I knew then that my being there was a mistake. There was nothing I could say or do that would change his mind. It was in his face.

"It is not uncomfortable here," he said, looking around.

There was a small fire going in a cresset. There was a pallet on the floor. The place was more of a room than a cell, and warm, considering the cold outside.

"I'll be free within days. Have no fear for me. Give the others my blessing."

The sergeant began to rattle his keys. There were sounds farther down the corridor.

I backed out of the room. "Keep my cloak," I said to Tyndale, tossing it to him.

The sergeant and I walked down the corridor.

"I may want to come back again. With more clothes," I said, giving him another sovereign. "Right now I wish you would let me out a side door, a back door, any door but the front door. There are those in the street who would like to do me a disfavor."

The sergeant led me to a back passage, and I circled the jail and came up behind the company concealed among the trees, waiting for the door to open.

With few words we broke up, there being night guards on the street, and made our way, one by one, quickly homeward.

Chapter 38

The next morning, perhaps as a result of the night before, Tyndale was transferred from the old jail in Antwerp to Vilvoorde, some seven leagues distant.

Vilvoorde was a small village on the outskirts of Brussels, with rich farmlands on all sides, a large marketplace, and a winding river, the Senne, that made a half loop around it.

In the center of this loop of swift-running water was a prison. It was really a castle built a century and a half before by one of the dukes of Brabant upon the model of the Bastille in Paris.

The prison had fortresslike walls, firing slits for windows, deep dungeons, trap doors from which hot lead could be poured upon those below, three moats spanned by drawbridges, and seven towers that surveyed aspects of the countryside for miles in all directions. It had been built by the duke as a refuge against his enemies. It was now the most impregnable fortress in the Low Countries—an ideal place to keep important prisoners.

This was why William Tyndale was taken to Vilvoorde to be tried as a heretic. He could never escape from Vilvoorde. An army could not rescue him.

But they didn't know what I suspected—that he wouldn't have tried to escape from even so much as an unguarded hut.

I was there for only the beginning of the trial, the whole of which lasted a year and a half. But I am told that the beginning was like the middle and that the middle was like the ending.

On the first day the important personages of the Lowlands were present. It was a bigger gathering of the rich and mighty than had attended Martin Luther's trial in Worms. There were processions and banners and bugles. William Tyndale, standing alone in his scholar's gown, a gray speck in all the glittering splendor, looked out of place.

The second day was not so stately and splendid. Clerks and attendants and barristers were flying everywhere. The trial was more like a child's toy that had been wound up and set down and allowed to rattle about here and there until it finally ran down.

I noticed one thing, however, in all the excitement and movement and talk. The court was presented with two Bibles. One was the Bible I had loaned to Phillips and which he had not returned. (I knew it from a water stain on the cover.) The other was a Bible translated into Flemish so that it could be read in court and understood; translated, I am certain, from my own English Bible.

That Phillips would stoop to this act, to use my Bible, the one I had read to him when he was sick, as a weapon against Tyndale did not surprise me. Yet it angered me to the point of a blind and rash act that could have caused my destruction.

After the third week of the trial, when it became clear that the verdict had already been decided and all that remained was a chance for various scholars to air their views, to steal a moment or so of attention, I set out for London, taking with me Ed Groat, Juan de Palos, and a pick-up crew of four.

I had no plans other than by some device, in some way, to gain an audience with the King.

Henry VIII was not in the mood to worry about anything except his own troubles. Efforts to rid himself of Catherine of Aragon and wed Anne Boleyn were first in his thoughts. He was on bad terms with Margaret, the Queen Regent, on even worse terms with Charles V, whom he blamed for holding up his divorce from Catherine.

But there was no time to wait for his mood to improve.

I first thought of going to Belsey, but gave this up in favor of Carswell at Clink. My funds were getting low, but I dug deep and came up with enough money to interest him in my project. His influence was such that within three days I was in the King's anteroom, waiting for an audience.

The King was sitting in a chair, a leg propped up on a sofa, heavily bandaged and thrust out in front of him. I remembered the young athlete, glowing with health, pacing the deck of the barge. It was a shock to see the same man now, bloated and sick and ill-humored.

"What is it?" he said. "It is something, else you wouldn't be here. A prebend, perhaps?" he added jokingly.

"It is about William Tyndale and the trial at Vilvoorde," I answered, too angry to carry on the joke, which would have been a saner course.

"I know of Tyndale and his troubles," the King said. "I have written a letter to the Queen Regent in protest. It is there by now. An outrage, typical of treatment meted out in the Low Countries. I will free Tyndale if I can. I would like to take an army to Vilvoorde and do it. They seem to think their fortress impervious to shot and shell. I'd like to show them that it's not. They have it coming, the stubborn pigs."

The audience ended when of a sudden he let forth a moan and his chamberlain rushed in, motioning me out. But I left with the feeling that the letter His Majesty had written to the Queen Regent might have an effect.

I had heard that the King, although he differed with Tyndale about many things, still had come to admire him and would like very much to have him back in England, if only to ask him to recant.

It was likewise rumored that his mistress, Anne Boleyn, favored Tyndale, had even read his New Testament, liked it and had given it to the King to read, who also found things to like in it.

Whatever the truth, we went back to Antwerp, then by horseback to Vilvoorde. The toy was winding down. Pierre Dufief, the procurator-general and a fearful little man, was tired. Scholars were still droning away in Latin, but they were running out of breath too.

Tyndale was offered the services of an advocate and a proctor, but he declined them both, saying that he would answer for himself, which he did simply and in a few words by saying that his life and his work were the answers. Like Luther, he had taken a stand and could do no other.

Henry VIII's letter reached the Queen Regent. She dutifully considered it but turned it down, as did the mighty Charles V. Neither of them was friendly with Henry at that time, unfortunately.

Tyndale was sent back to prison to await the verdict.

I had my ship to care for and a crew to pay. I made two voyages of six months each to Sumatra and several shorter voyages, but whenever it was possible I went to see William Tyndale. He was not in a dungeon, though they had many. The commander of Vilvoorde was not ill-disposed toward Tyndale, but Tyndale was a prisoner, a heretic, and thousands of eyes were upon him.

A letter Tyndale gave me to give to the commander of the prison is a sign of his plight while the trial was going on. The letter read:

> I believe, right worshipful, that you are not unaware of what may have been determined concerning me. Wherefore I beg your lordship, and that by the Lord Jesus, that if I am to remain here through the winter, you will request the commissary to have the kindness to send me, from the goods of mine which he has, a warmer cap; for I suffer greatly from cold in the head; a warmer coat also, for this which I have is very thin; a piece of cloth too to patch my leggings. My overcoat is worn out; my shirts are also worn out. He has a woolen shirt, if he will be good enough to send it. I have also with him leggings of thicker cloth to put on above; he has also warmer nightcaps.
>
> And I ask to be allowed to have a lamp in the evening; it is indeed wearisome sitting alone in the dark. But most of all I beg and beseech your clemency to be urgent with the commissary, that he will kindly permit me to have the Hebrew bible, Hebrew grammar, and Hebrew dictionary, that I may pass the time in that study. In return may you obtain what you most desire, so only that it be for the salvation of your soul.
>
> But if any other decision has been taken concerning me, to be carried out before winter, I will be patient, abiding the will of God, to the glory of the grace of my Lord Jesus Christ; whose Spirit (I pray) may ever direct your heart. Amen.
>
> W. Tyndale

The letter must have been read by somebody in the prison, but Tyndale never received his cloak nor shirt nor candle.

Early in August of the next year, having spent a winter in his dark, bitterly cold cell, he was condemned as a heretic, degraded from the priesthood, and handed over to the secular power for punishment.

Chapter 39

The punishment was expected within a week of the sentence. It occurred nearly two months later in the village of Vilvoorde.

I heard about the punishment while I was in Antwerp. I rode all night with Juan de Palos and Ed Groat to be there. It was the worst night of my life.

The hanging of William Tyndale took place at the hour of nine in the morning.

In front of Vilvoorde Castle and on the outskirts of the village was a marketplace. On the side closest to the prison, which was part of the village marketplace, they had built a large circle enclosed by a wooden barricade, which was guarded. The townspeople, most of whom had already been to market and were carrying baskets of vegetables and fruit, were gathered around the barricade.

Inside the barricade were two great beams set up in the shape of a cross, as tall as a tall man. Chains were fastened to the top, and there were two holes through which ran a hemp rope. Brushwood and logs and hay lay scattered around.

The procurator-general, the commander of the prison, and their colleagues sat on benches made especially for them.

Tyndale was brought in, dressed in his threadbare gown, and for the last time was asked to recant. He said nothing and moved to the cross. His feet were bound to the driven stake with hemp. The chain was looped around his neck, as was a loose length of the hempen rope. Then the brushwood and logs and also a portion of gunpowder were packed around his feet.

The edifice looked like a little hut put up in the wilderness for the comfort of weary travelers. And that it may have been for William Tyndale.

I was close enough to the guarded barricade to see his face. He looked to me like a man who had taken a long journey, who was tired, and at last had found a place to rest.

I don't know that he saw me, though I was a head taller than those around me and could clearly see him. But there was a gentle look in his eyes, a look of hope and love, and I like to think that it was meant for me.

The procurator-general, a benign man of pleasant countenance, then gave a signal to the executioner, whose arms were folded across his chest and who stood partly behind the cross. Quickly the executioner tightened the hempen noose.

While there was still breath in him, Tyndale spoke clearly, so all could hear. His dying prayer was, "Lord, open the King of England's eyes."

Now that the prisoner's life was ended, the procurator grasped a wax torch and handed it to the executioner, who reached down and set the gunpowder ablaze.

The fire went fiercely. It was a bright October day with a strong wind blowing and the brushwood and logs did not take long to burn.

All that was left was a small handful of ashes.

I walked to the barricade, thinking that I would gather the ashes, but a guard turned me back with the butt of his musket.

Ed Groat, Juan de Palos, and I walked along the edge of the river. The water was low and everywhere you could see the stones on the bottom and small fish gliding among them like blue shadows.

Juan de Palos said, "Let us go to find Henry Phillips."

"Let us go," Ed Groat said, and I repeated the words.

Our horses were grazing beside the river. We saddled them and rode back to Antwerp. We were the first to bring the news of our friend's death.

The church bells were ringing as we rode out of the city toward Amsterdam, where Phillips was said to be. But he was not in Amsterdam.

We needed to make a voyage to London and by chance passed the Tower as the mighty boom of a cannon rocked the ship. We were to learn later that it signalled the moment Anne Boleyn was beheaded and the King was free to marry his next wife.

In late November we got news that Phillips had passed through Germany and was on his way to Rome.

A letter of Henry the Eighth, now in better health, reached the English ambassador there as Phillips was making friends and preparing some doubtful scheme. He was driven from Rome, by the King's letter, to Paris, to Venice, and then I received word from Sarah Williams that he was back in Antwerp.

Chapter 40

We were in London when the word came. We sailed for Antwerp that day, and I went at once to see Sarah Williams, taking Ed Groat and Juan de Palos along.

It was midday, and she was sitting with her friends around a pot of stew in the cold loft near the waterfront.

"He's here," Sarah Williams said. "He came last week without so much as shoes or a cloak."

"Why?" I asked. "To see Poyntz? Poyntz has Tyndale's papers."

"No, Poyntz took them to the Adventurers' warehouse."

"Do you suppose that Phillips will try to get the papers? There must be a bundle."

"He might. It could be the reason he's here."

It was raining hard, and the rain was coming down through cracks in the roof. Where the water dripped the heaviest, they had placed pots and pans. Now and then someone would get up and toss the water through the window.

"We should go to the Other World," Juan de Palos said. "There it rains but the sun shines and there is fruit to eat of all kinds, and many fish to catch."

"We have things to do first," Ed Groat said.

Juan de Palos was persistent. He must have learned his persistence from Columbus. "Mistress Sarah can be the turner of the sand and keep us informed of the time."

"Where shall we look for Phillips?" Ed Groat said.

"He could be on your ship," Sarah Williams said.

"We have two men posted," I answered. "That will serve to keep him away."

"Then he could be at the warehouse," Sarah Williams said. "That's where Tyndale's papers are now. Don't forget that he has friends among the Adventurers."

I looked at Ed Groat, and he nodded.

We left the garret, tumbling down the stairs in our hurry. The rain had ceased, but a shrill cold wind was blowing in from the sea.

We could see the sky aglow when we were still a league away. By the time we reached the Adventurers' main warehouse, it was on fire. The roof had tumbled in, and only the stone walls stood. Men had buckets in their hands, but they had given up and were standing idly around. Nothing but ashes remained within the stone walls.

We met Phillips by chance on our way back to the ship. It was at an inn we frequented when in the city, noted for its seafood and its absence of fustylugs.

There was a huge fire burning, and he was standing in front of it. He was blue with cold and a mere shadow of the gallant I remembered from London.

Juan de Palos was the first to speak. "We have a score to settle, I think," he said. "Do you wish that we settle it here or outside, where you can hear nothing except the cold wind blowing?"

"It is all settled," Phillips said.

"Some of it but not all," I said.

"I do not like the wind very much," Juan said. "Do you like the wind, Señor Tomas?"

"No," I answered. "Less even than what we now see in front of us."

Phillips stood leaning against the fireplace, steam coming from his ragged clothes, even what remained of his shoes.

"He is unarmed," Ed Groat said.

"If he had a six-foot double blade, it would do him no good," said Juan. "I will slit his throat quietly and push him into the fire."

"That should warm him," Ed Groat said.

Under his doublet he had a club that would fell an ox. Lacking a club, he could attend to the matter with one blow of his fist.

We had followed Phillips a long way, for a long time, heard many rumors of him, made many threats against his life. And here he was, at last, standing on the hearth of a inn where death was a common thing, within the length of an arm, the reach of a blade. We talked, yet not one of us moved.

Juan de Palos looked Phillips slowly up and down. He took his Toledo blade from its leather shield. Then he glanced at me for a sign. I gave him none.

In place of Phillips standing there at the hearth, I saw William Tyndale tied to a brushwood fire. I saw his eyes looking out at the clear-running river and the marketplace and the crowd with its bounteous baskets and the benches filled with dignitaries in their medals and colored ribbons. I saw him glancing calmly at the sky and the river, at all of us.

"What became of your friend Belsey?" I asked Phillips.

"Dead of the plague," was the chattering answer.

"Why did you burn the warehouse?" I asked.

"To put an end to all of William Tyndale's heretical scribbles."

Phillips' hands were blue with cold. Steam came still from his tattered clothes. I wore a warm cloak and he wore none, but I was not enough of a Christian to give him mine. If Tyndale were here now—not here in my thoughts, but here alive—he would have given Phillips his cloak, if he had one to give. Of this I was certain.

"The words William Tyndale wrote and gave his life for you cannot burn," I said. "Your fires lighted the sky but nothing else."

Juan de Palos rubbed the Toledo blade against the top of his leather boot, turned the blade over and rubbed the other side. He was still looking at me, waiting for the sign.

In the pocket of my cloak were a few small coins. I walked over to Phillips and put them into his palm, which was more like a claw than a human hand. I did not look at Ed Groat nor at Juan de Palos.

I left Phillips there at the hearth with his rags and his lice and soleless boots and went out into the street. Juan de Palos and Ed Groat silently followed me. We bent our heads against the storm. The street was deserted, and the houses were dark, except for one where a celebration was taking place. There were lanterns in its windows and in the garden. They cast a glow upon our path.

Nothing was said, but the three of us stopped as if by consent. I could see the faces of Ed Groat and Juan de Palos in the shadowed light. They still were filled with puzzlement at me, at what I had done, at what I had failed to do.

Juan de Palos took his knife out of its sheath and rubbed it on his sleeve.

"It is not too late, señor," he said.

"I think William Tyndale would think so," I answered. "I think he would have chosen this way."

Ed Groat said, "It is possible."

We started off again. At the end of the street, through the bare branches of the trees, I could see the beckoning light of our ship.

Author's Note

The principal characters in this story, except Tom Barton, the narrator, and his Uncle Jack, are people of history, including King Henry VIII, Sir Thomas More, John Stokesley, Peter Quentel the printer, Peter Schoeffer the printer, Johann Dobneck, Hermann Rinck, Henry Phillips, Thomas Poyntz, and William Tyndale himself. Two others, Herbert Belsey and Samuel Carswell, are based upon real characters.

Smuggling is an important part of the story. In the time of Henry it was not so infrequent as it is now—we have invented more varied and sophisticated types of fraud. Towns, cities, districts, whole lengths of the English coast were engaged in smuggling.

It was not only a profitable and a fairly honorable profession but also a source of adventure for the old and the young. It began in the thirteenth century and came to flower 400 years later under Samuel Pepys. As Secretary of the Admiralty, Pepys made a tidy fortune by outfitting ships seized from the Dutch and French and sending them forth as his own armed privateers to prey upon foreign commerce.

The plague described in the story was known as the Black Death. It took several forms, most of them fatal. It commonly came from a virus carried by rats or their fleas. The disease appeared suddenly. A person might be alive at breakfast and dead by suppertime. In the fourteenth century, when the plague was at its height, one-fourth of the population of Europe, or some 25,000,000 persons, died of this epidemic.

William Tyndale was forced to flee England and for eleven years hid in peril of his life from the secret agents of the Crown and the Church. He hid so successfully that there are several years of this period when no one knows where he hid. Even today, after years of diligent search, his hiding places, wherever they were, whether in the Low Countries, in France, or in Germany, are still unknown.

I have followed Tyndale's life as it is set down by the best known of his biographers, J. F. Mozley and C. H. Williams. Tyndale's letter to the Governor of Vilvoorde Castle, asking for a warmer shirt, a Hebrew Bible, and a candle to read by, is word for word the letter Tyndale wrote.

Tyndale's wish was to translate the New Testament from its original Greek into everyday English. In the words of Erasmus of Rotterdam, speaking of the Gospels, he wished "that the plowman might sing parts of them at his plow and the weaver at his shuttle, and that the traveler might beguile with their narration the weariness of his way."

His perilous life lasted long enough for him to fulfill this wish.